Without really thinking about it, Callum opened his mouth and made words of his own.

"Talking you me to?" he asked numbly, not getting the words in the proper order, which was understandable. He was pretty rusty at it.

"Of *course* I'm talking to *you*. Who *else* would it be?" the strange woman bellowed in reply. For that's what she was, Callum suddenly knew. She wasn't an animal at all, but a woman. And the other animals were people, and he was a human too.

I'm smart! he thought proudly. And not just with sticks and termites. Future Alpha material, no doubt about it.

The Boy Who Howled

TIMOTHY POWER

BLOOMSBURY

NEW YORK BERLIN LONDON SYDNEY

For my mom and
all moms everywhere

First published in the United States of America in October 2010
by Bloomsbury Books for Young Readers
Paperback edition published in June 2012
www.bloomsburykids.com

For information about permission to reproduce selections from this book, write to
Permissions, Bloomsbury BFYR, 175 Fifth Avenue, New York, New York 10010

The Library of Congress has cataloged the hardcover edition as follows:
Power, Timothy.
The boy who howled / by Timothy Power. — 1st U.S. ed.
p.   cm.
Summary: A boy who has been raised by wolves from a young age unexpectedly finds himself
back in human society, trying to figure out how to fit in.
ISBN 978-1-59990-509-9 (hardcover)
1. Humorous stories. [1. Feral children—Fiction. 2. Wolves—Fiction. 3. Twins—Fiction.
4. Schools—Fiction. 5. Families—Fiction.] I. Title.
PZ7.P88282Bo 2010   [Fic]—dc22   2010003474

ISBN 978-1-59990-852-6 (paperback)

Book design by Donna Mark
Typeset by Westchester Book Composition
Printed in the U.S.A. by Quad/Graphics, Fairfield, Pennsylvania
2 4 6 8 10 9 7 5 3 1

All papers used by Bloomsbury Publishing, Inc., are natural, recyclable products
made from wood grown in well-managed forests. The manufacturing processes
conform to the environmental regulations of the country of origin.

FIRST, A WORD FROM AN EXPERT

"Wolves are some of the most ferocious predators on the planet. Sure, they can be nice sometimes, even friendly. I've seen them grin and wag their tails like the family dog. But they will bring down and rip to pieces a bull moose without so much as a how-do-you-do, and I'm not just whistling 'Dixie.' I wouldn't get too close, if I were you. In fact, I wouldn't go anywhere near 'em. They'll rip off your head as soon as look at you."

—World-famous wildlife wrangler Buzz "I Could Smell Really Well Before That Angry Porcupine Ripped Off My Nose" Optigon

The Boy Who Howled

CHAPTER ONE

Callum in the Wild

A gentle snow was falling, dotting the forest floor with fleecy white. There wasn't a sound to be heard other than the crunch of dry twigs and pine needles under Callum's stiff knees as he crawled on all fours in what he hoped was the proper direction.

Somewhere up ahead, Mom and Dad were getting dinner, silently stalking a deer, or an elk, or a caribou. He hoped they weren't too far away. On their powerful legs and sturdy paws they could run like the wind. And he could only crawl so fast, especially on the hard, frozen, rocky ground.

He sighed, and his breath made a fluffy white cloud in the frigid air. He would have liked to help with dinner. He knew that Mom would come get him when the meal was ready, and he would gorge himself alongside the others on the steaming raw meat—but just once he would like to join in when Dad sprang at the prey, clamped his jaws on its defenseless throat, and, ripping and snarling, choked the very life out of it, while Mom chomped down hard on one of its vulnerable rear legs.

Callum was the youngest member of the pack, and he wasn't at all prepared to do anything as ferocious as that. But he could throw a rock like a pro, and he could beat the deer, or the elk, or the caribou with his fists after it was brought down, if he was given the opportunity. At the very least, it would tenderize the meat, which was always tough and stringy.

Not that anyone else in the pack noticed that. He was the only one who bothered to chew his food. The others simply tore off enormous chunks of it with their razor-sharp incisors and gulped the pieces whole. Luckily he never needed more than a mouthful or two to fill his stomach, because that's all that was left after the tearing and gulping was over. Mom, Dad, Aunt Trudy, Uncle Rick, and even snaggle-toothed old Grampa could strip a full-grown elk's carcass to the bone in a matter of minutes. They saved a lot of time by not chewing.

There was nothing polite about dinnertime. Even Mom, who usually had very good manners for a North American Gray Wolf or Timber Wolf (*Canis lupus*), would growl and snap like crazy if anyone came near her portion of food. By the time the feasting was over, however, pretty much everyone was in a really good mood. Drowsy, stuffed, burping, and farting, the whole pack quickly settled down for bed in their den in the crevice of the mountainside.

Callum would curl up between Mom and Aunt Trudy. This was Mom's idea, due to the fact that even though Callum had spent so much time with the pack, Dad still wanted to devour him. Before he fell asleep he would press his face against Mom's two-layered coat and inhale the homey scents of oily musk and ruminant innards. Her outer coat of guard hairs, which repelled dirt and water, was rough and scratchy, but her dense, soft undercoat kept him warm and cozy.

Dad, Uncle Rick, and Grampa sometimes kicked their legs in their sleep as if they were running or chasing another dinner. Now and then they even howled a little, reminding Callum of the times when the whole family gathered in the early evenings under the rising moon and howled their lungs out. Things didn't get any more fun than that.

When everyone was howling together, Callum really felt like one of the family and not some fangless outsider. Every belly was full of raw, bloody meat, so nobody thought about killing anyone. Dad would sometimes pee on him, to mark him with his scent, and Mom would seem to smile, and everything would be right with the world. Aunt Trudy and Uncle Rick stopped complaining long enough to listen to Grampa tell stories of the long-ago days when so many of his relatives roamed the woods that he couldn't squat under a bush to relieve himself without booting someone out before he could get the job done.

"Needless to say, that was before someone else's relatives showed up and kicked us all to the curb," he would complain with a frown, then look at Callum accusingly, and the whole pack, including Mom, would start to growl at him, and Callum could tell that Dad was thinking about devouring him again.

Grampa didn't speak in words, of course. In fact, none of the family spoke at all, in the strictest sense. Still, they were communicating all the time, and Callum always seemed to know exactly what they were saying. How? Well, for one thing, he used his imagination. And for another, it was pretty hard to mistake an angry growl for anything else. Whatever the reason for it, he certainly seemed to understand the call of the Wild.

Unfortunately, when he tried to talk to *them*, the family hardly ever understood a single thing he said. Whenever he barked and yipped and yapped at them, they would look at him funny and roll their eyes. Only when he howled did they really get the drift of what he was trying to get across, and howling was reserved for special occasions only. So when he got up the nerve to ask in his own language who these other relatives were, exactly, and what they had against Grampa's relatives, all that came out, at least to Grampa's ears, was a weird kind of groan that sounded like "Who them?" and ended with a hiccup.

Grampa narrowed his eyes and barked, and Callum imagined he said, "Once again, I can hardly understand a single word that comes out of your mouth, Firehead, and if you ask me, that's a big part of the problem with the world today right there."

And Callum felt strangely guilty, and he wanted to howl, but it wasn't allowed because it wasn't a special occasion. So he simply whimpered and rolled over onto his back instead, exposing his vulnerable throat and underside.

Mom and Dad always appreciated it when he did that. Even Aunt Trudy and Uncle Rick stopped complaining about what a burden he was when he was flat on his back with his arms and legs in the air.

Grampa only scoffed at him this time. "Save that kind of behavior for the Alphas and the Betas, why don't you?" he seemed to say in a low and steady growl. "I'm the Omega member of this pack, the bottom of the bunch. Though you'd probably be the Omega yourself if you possessed so much as a hint of a tail, and I'd be sitting pretty. As it is, I have no idea what your status is in the pecking order around here. I suppose you're just a furless mascot, which means that you're out of the loop altogether."

It was obvious that none of the rest of the family had the slightest idea where Callum fit in either, although Mom would sometimes call him her little Pig Face or Salty Lollipop. At least, he imagined she did.

To Dad, of course, he was more like dinner than anything else. There was no mistaking the voracious gleam in those glittering yellow eyes, or the buckets of foamy saliva that poured from his jowls whenever Dad looked at him. But Callum didn't take it to heart. Everything reminded Dad of dinner. And Dad wasn't the only one. The whole family was continually thinking of dinner. In fact, when Mom and Dad first came across Callum crawling alone and defenseless in the woods who knows how long ago, it was plain to see that the first thought that came into both of their heads was to kill him and eat him, or eat him alive. But as luck would have it, they had just gorged themselves on an entire family of defenseless rabbits that they had managed to trap in a hollow log nearby, and so they couldn't swallow another bite.

Callum didn't know it, but it was even luckier for him that he chose that very moment to roll over onto his back and wave his arms and legs in the air. He didn't plan it or anything. It was just something he enjoyed doing.

Mom must have appreciated this textbook display of submissive behavior, because she stopped Dad from ripping out his insides. "I don't care how tasty he looks. He's polite, he's only a cub, and he's mine, and nobody is going to tear him to pieces," she had declared possessively. Dad was left to snarl and snap his fearsome jaws in frustration, but he allowed her to take Callum back to the den, most likely because he planned to devour him later.

Nobody was more surprised to see Callum show up at the pack's crowded crevice in the rocky mountainside than Aunt Trudy and Uncle Rick—who immediately started complaining about it—unless it was Grampa, whose startled expression certainly said, "Wrap me up in moose beards and spank me with a pinecone! I never thought I'd see the day when I would share a den with the likes of that!"

"If he isn't dinner, he's just another mouth to feed," grumbled Aunt Trudy, curling her lip in disdain. "Does anyone seriously think we can afford it?"

"One whiff of him and there won't be an elk around for miles," griped Uncle Rick, wrinkling his nose. "I don't look forward to eating nothing but red squirrels and black beetles for the foreseeable future. Yuck! He's already stinking up the den. He smells like . . . *lilacs*."

"I'll take care of that right now," said Dad with a sensible snort and then lifted his leg, which marked the first time that he ever peed on Callum.

"That's so much better," agreed the rest of the family with a few contented yips when he was done, and then Mom regurgitated a bit of half-digested rabbit onto the ground for Callum to eat, and everybody settled down to sleep.

The last things Callum saw before he dropped off to dreamland were Dad's yellow eyes glowing in the dark, staring him right in the face.

Every night after that, Mom made sure that he slept between her and Aunt Trudy. "Nobody's going to devour my little Pig Face," she seemed to say fondly in his imagination, licking his cheek with her sandpaper tongue. "Though I've got to admit, you do taste good. Yum!"

From that point on, every new day was a learning experience. Week after week, month after month, Callum worked hard to master the ways of the pack while trying not to look too delicious. Whenever he wanted to get anywhere, he crawled on his hands and knees in order to appear more like a family member. Although he could never keep up with the others, he was never too far behind. He grew accustomed to eating his food as raw as it came, generously dusted with dirt and hair, and every once in a while, when the pack got together in the early evenings to howl their lungs out at the rising moon, he howled louder than anyone.

His knees grew more and more sore from crawling around on rocks and twigs until he got used to it, sort of. Every night for at least two whole months he dropped off to sleep as soon as his weary eyes were shut.

But all of that was a long time ago. These days he could safely say he was pretty well used to the daily grind of life in the Wild. Still, however hard he tried to fit in, he never felt like he truly belonged in the world of woodland creatures. Now and then, as he lay in bed listening to Dad and Aunt Trudy snoring like there was no tomorrow, he wondered how on earth he had ended up sharing a den in a crevice on a mountainside with five such vicious (and noisy!) companions.

There was a vague recollection in the back of his mind that he had come from a gentler place, where he had been able to speak and be understood by others. He could make out shadowy shapes of dinners like him at the back of his mind, and hear some of the things that they said.

"You're a smart boy, all right," one of the shadowy figures said proudly. "What a brain! You're like a toddler encyclopedia."

"You're my pudding and pie," another shadowy figure said lovingly. "One of the two brightest lights of my life."

But he didn't like to think of these shadowy figures because he was mad at them for some reason. Furious, really. And the bulk of what they said was pure mush.

There was another voice in his head, and he heard it loud and clear. This was his own language, and it was what allowed him to imagine what Mom, Dad, Aunt Trudy, Uncle Rick, and Grampa seemed to be saying. But as for where he learned it, he must have hit his head on a rock or something and forgotten about it, because his only memory of it was a horrible period of time that he spent crying his eyes out, when he felt so lonely and forgotten that he thought he was the only living thing in the whole of creation.

That was right before he met Mom and Dad in the clearing.

"Where did I come from?" he attempted to ask Mom one night before bedtime, contorting the Pig Face that she loved so dearly into what he hoped was a questioning look.

Of course, to Mom's ears all that came out of him was the same weird kind of groan as always, as well as something that sounded vaguely like "Where me was?" followed by a hiccup.

But by some stroke of luck, this time it seemed that she actually understood him. At least he imagined she did.

"You showed up out of nowhere, my little Pig Face," she answered with a loving smile that showed off her razor-sharp teeth and healthy gums. "You fell right into my lap. And I couldn't be happier with my little Salty Lollipop!"

Then she licked his cheek a few hundred times with her sandpaper tongue, which brought the grand total of licks to at least a million.

"Ouch!" he cried nervously, and she gave him another enormous toothy grin, her yellow eyes glittering. Leaping to her feet, she brought him an old argyle sock from her stash of things behind a rock.

Mom was a scavenger. She was always picking up weird items from her travels through the woods and hiding them in the den. Now and then she'd pull out a few things to give as gifts to Dad, Aunt Trudy, Uncle Rick, and Grampa. Once she brought out a floppy piece of rubber that the voice in Callum's mind told him was a bicycle tire, of all things.

One night not long ago, she had returned to the den carrying a bulging rucksack in her teeth. Looking inside it, Callum discovered a full set of clothes that fit him well enough, although he had never worn a dress before. It appeared that Mom didn't approve of his going around naked.

"You're appetizing enough as it is," she explained with a worried glance toward Dad. "I don't want anyone to think that you've become a walking hamburger."

The clothes smelled thrillingly of something Callum knew he had sniffed before, but he couldn't remember where or when.

"That's campfire smoke," complained Aunt Trudy, wrinkling her nose and bristling all over. "Smelling that is definitely not good for my nerves. I'm already on edge after getting kicked in the head by that caribou today."

"You're on edge?" griped Uncle Rick in a pitiful whine. "Try ripping one of those things to pieces when your paw has a cramp. Now it hurts more than ever. I've got Caribou Cramp."

Dad was even more upset. He paced back and forth in the den with an angry restlessness. "I don't like you risking your neck over something so foolish," he seemed to complain, snarling at Mom. "What does your precious furless mascot need clothes for, anyway? We're going to devour him sooner or later, aren't we?"

"Relax," she replied, licking his snout reassuringly. "The campsite was only ten miles away. I ran all the way there and back, and I'm not even winded."

Grampa spent the rest of the night trying to chew up Callum's old set of clothes but ended up mainly drooling all over them.

"Our kind were kings and queens once," he seemed to say mournfully with a series of quivering grunts and groans, a soggy tangle of cotton threads dangling from his jaws. "We were worshipped like gods. Everyone knew we had mystical powers. Now we're on the run, only two steps ahead of total extinction."

"Quit your yapping, old man," snapped Dad, baring his teeth. "We're trying to get some sleep here."

"That's right," grumbled Uncle Rick, putting his ears back. "Those of us who actually pull our weight on a kill have got to get some shut-eye."

Grampa muttered one last thing and then settled down to sleep. Chances were good that what he said was not at all polite.

"Goodnight, my little Pig Face," whispered Mom, licking Callum's red, raw cheek once more. "Sweet dreams, my Salty Lollipop. See you in the morning."

Callum lay in the dark and wondered what a campfire might be. Shouldn't he know? The word had come from his own mind, after all. But he didn't think very long or hard about it. He was so tired from crawling around all day on his hands and knees on the hard, rocky ground that he was sound asleep in two seconds flat.

CHAPTER TWO

Callum, Out of the Wild

The following day, Callum was once again crawling on his hands and knees on the hard, frozen, rocky ground, determined to catch up with the pack. Once more, delicate flakes of snow began to drift from the thick, fluffy clouds overhead. The gentle snow became a flurry, and then it began to come down so fast that the forest floor was quickly covered in white.

Soon Callum could no longer tell where the white ground ended and the white sky began. He stopped crawling and sat back on his haunches. It wouldn't do any good to head off in the wrong direction. Mom could whiff him out wherever he was, but she was never very happy if she had to go out of her way, especially when dinner was ready.

The thought of dinner made Callum's empty stomach rumble. He had snacked on some spicy termites that he'd come across in an old rotten tree stump, but that was hours ago. They were so peppery that his tongue still felt kind of numb. He pulled a pine needle from under the snow and used it to remove an itchy termite leg that was stuck between his teeth.

So what if he would never be any good at lunging at a deer, or an elk, or a caribou, and ripping out its throat? There were other ways that he could make himself useful to the pack. His chief advantage was the fact that he had hands instead of paws. He could lift things when he needed to, and use pointy sticks as tools, like he had done earlier that day to poke out his meal of termites through the hole in the tree stump. Not even an Alpha Male like Dad could do that.

In fact, now that he thought about it, if any of the family got a hankering for a snack of greasy, spicy termites, he could definitely make their wish come true. He was just imagining dishing up a mouthwatering portion of the soft-bodied insects for Dad when he caught sight of Mom.

She had crept up as silently as the snowfall and was looking at him with concern in her glittering yellow eyes. There was a grim sort of tightness around her blood-flecked muzzle, as if she had some really bad news to tell him. It worried him. He would have liked it if she licked his cheek for reassurance, even if it threatened to take the skin off, but she just continued to frown at him and clench her jaws. A million anxious thoughts raced through his mind. Had something happened to Dad? Aunt Trudy? Uncle Rick? Grampa?

"Dinner's ready," she seemed to say at long last with a shake of her muscular head.

Dinner! In his thoughts of termite retrieval and concern for the pack, Callum had almost forgotten about it. Even at the sound of the word, his stomach reverberated with the same kind of noises that Grampa's intestines made in the middle of the night.

He was as hungry as, well, a wolf.

"It's just a mule deer, dear," he imagined Mom say as she took a hard look at the bleak wintry landscape. "A juvenile, I'm afraid. Nothing to get excited about. More like an appetizer than a proper meal. Still, it's better than nothing."

She began to walk back toward the woods. Callum got down on all fours and followed her. To his surprise, he found that he had grown so much lately that even on his hands and knees he stood nearly shoulder-to-shoulder to Mom. Mom appeared to notice it too, and she didn't seem very happy about it.

The snowfall had pretty much stopped by the time they reached the dinner table. For a juvenile, the mule deer had obviously put up quite a fight. Aunt Trudy was sporting a fresh bruise on her head, and Uncle Rick was sadly nursing his cramped paw.

Grampa snorted impatiently as Callum and Mom stepped through the brush. "Finally!" he seemed to say. "It's about time. We can say grace."

"Oh Great Spirit that guides the Sun and Moon and Lights the Stars and watches over All That Lives in This World and Beyond," began Dad, looking up at the sky with all due respect, "we thank You for this nourishing meal, although You had less to do with it than I did after that darn deer gave Trudy another good kick in the head and Rick there wasted all our time with a few pathetic scratches when he should have been savagely clawing its guts out. We wouldn't have anything at all to eat if I hadn't ripped its head clean off with a single blow from my powerful paws. This pack would be nowhere without me. Nowhere!"

And with that, he glared at Callum fiercely.

"All right, dear, we get it," Mom seemed to say with a soft, nervous whine, but Dad kept glaring at Callum so fiercely that Callum felt obliged to roll over onto his back and expose his throat one more time.

"There he goes again!" scoffed Grampa. "Enough of this jibber-jabber. Let's eat!"

The whole family rushed at the carcass in a blur of blood and gore and mule deer hide. But whenever Callum came forward to claim his share, Dad lunged at him and snapped his teeth so ferociously that he fell down and rolled over onto his back again.

A few minutes later there was hardly any mule deer left, and Callum was as hungry as he was before dinner started.

"Here," said Grampa, sidling up to him so that Dad wouldn't notice. "I saved you something."

He dropped a mouthful of spleen and a smidgen of pancreas near Callum's head. It could be that he hadn't meant to. He might have done it by accident. But he didn't seem to want it back. He looked away and lashed his spindly tail.

"Thanks, Grampa," Callum said and quickly devoured the slimy bites, but of course all Grampa heard was a weird kind of groan and hiccuppy sound.

"You're lucky I'm around, Firehead," he barked, running his ragged pink tongue gingerly along the worn-down stumps of his ancient chompers. "If it were up to the big guy, you'd have been stuck with the tail. And goodness knows there isn't much meat on a mule deer's tail, especially when it's a juvenile and only an appetizer to begin with."

Callum looked over at Dad, who was gnawing on a rib bone for all he was worth.

What had happened? he wondered. Had he done something to make Dad unhappy? If only he had been able to help out with the hunt! He looked forward to getting the opportunity to show Dad what he could do with a stick for a tool and a bunch of termites in an old rotten log. He could also carry some of the leftover mule deer bones back to the den, if there were any left over, although he would have to walk on two legs to do that. On second thought, it might not be worth it. Seeing him walk on two legs made Dad madder than anything.

He silently vowed to do whatever it took to make Dad proud enough to want to pee on him again.

Back at the den, the entire family seemed especially upset for some reason. Outside, the moon was on the rise, but nobody thought about howling. They were too busy growling and snapping at each other for that. As usual, Callum used his imagination to catch the drift of what was going on with them.

"My poor little Pig Face," Mom seemed to say, nudging him gently with her freezing wet snout. "My poor little Salty Lollipop. It's not your fault, exactly. You're growing so quickly is all. It's becoming a problem. You're a male, as you know. Dad is only doing what comes naturally. He expects he'll have to fight you any day now for supremacy over the pack."

"There's only room for one Alpha Male!" snapped Dad, who was pacing nearby. He was foaming at the muzzle, and the guard hairs bristled along his powerful back.

"There's only room for one Beta Male too!" piped up Uncle Rick.

"Omega is up for grabs, if anyone wants it," said Grampa, who then farted loudly. "Look out below! Man, does pancreas ever give me gas."

"We've come to a turning point for our furless mascot," snuffled Mom, looking at Callum with sadness in her glittering yellow eyes. "No one's to blame. It's Nature's way."

"Hooray for Nature!" declared Uncle Rick. "It's never let us down."

After what seemed like forever, the family settled down for bed. Dad walked in a circle at least a hundred times before hitting the sack.

"I was going to give this to you anyway, my little Pig Face," Mom whimpered, nosing another bulging rucksack from behind the rock.

Dad and Aunt Trudy, already asleep, were snoring loudly enough to bring the roof down.

"I would have brought it out earlier, but I didn't want Dad to know I'd gone back to the campsite," said Mom. "Honestly, I don't see why he makes such a big deal about it. Running there and back is a snap. The real problem is that stealing is wrong, but I just can't help myself. I'm a wild animal, after all."

Callum looked inside the bag and pulled out a white polo shirt, a pair of khaki pants, white socks, colorful briefs, and a navy blue blazer with a curious patch on the chest that featured some strange markings. Also, a small round button was pinned to the front of the jacket, and on it was a picture of what looked like a little tree that was growing upside-down.

By this time, he had a pretty good idea of what was going on. These were travel clothes. His days with the pack had come to an end. It was time he moved on.

I don't want to fight Dad for supremacy of the pack, he thought sadly. So I guess I'll have to go away. But where? Deeper into the forest, to live with the bears?

It was with a heavy heart that he lay down to sleep between Mom and Aunt Trudy that night, and Mom felt mournful too. He could tell by the way she kept interrupting her rest to lick his face off during the night.

[19]

His cheek was rubbed raw by the morning. Bright and early, Mom woke everyone up and made an announcement. Or at least he imagined she did.

"As you know, many winters have come and gone since Dad and I gorged ourselves on that family of defenseless rabbits that we trapped in the hollow log," she began, whimpering softly.

Dad's eyes misted over. "Man, they were tasty," he muttered nostalgically.

"I wish *I* had been lucky enough to devour a whole family of rabbits," remarked Aunt Trudy enviously.

"I'd have been happy to devour half a family of rabbits. I never get a break like that," pouted Uncle Rick.

"Rabbits, schmabbits," scoffed Grampa, turning up his nose at a source of food, for once. "Who needs 'em? Too much fluff for my taste. Makes me sneeze."

"Then we walked into the clearing," Mom went on. "And lo and behold, we saw something that really threw us for a loop. Dad wanted to devour him, and I did too, but we were so stuffed with delicious young rabbit that we couldn't eat another bite. And then all of a sudden he did the cutest thing . . . something dinner had never done before. He rolled over onto his back, exposing his vulnerable throat and underside. Yes, he assumed the submissive position to Dad. Well, I was never so touched by anything in my life, seeing a dinner do something like that, considering how often it simply screams its head off and begs for its life and then kicks Aunt Trudy in the head. I had always wanted a pet, and this dinner was looking cuter by the minute. So I persuaded Dad to let me keep him, and from that moment on we've enjoyed having a furless mascot in our den."

"A furless freeloader, more like it," grumbled Aunt Trudy, who was still smarting over Mom's crack about getting kicked in the head.

"And a smelly one," complained Uncle Rick. "Oh mighty Alpha, Ruler of the Den, please pee on him again."

Snorting scornfully, Dad refused to budge.

"As it has become all too plain to see these past few weeks," continued Mom with a yip and a bark, "my little Salty Lollipop has grown big enough to battle Dad for supe-riority of the pack or challenge Uncle Rick for Beta position."

"There's only room for one Alpha Male!" Dad snapped again.

"There's only room for one Beta Male too!" repeated Uncle Rick, snapping as well, although not as ferociously as Dad.

"I shouldn't have to say it again," barked Grampa, "but Omega is still up for grabs."

"My smart little Pig Face has decided not to compete with Dad and risk being torn limb from limb by Dad's razor-sharp teeth and deadly claws," Mom whimpered. "Neither does he want to be bruised by multiple thumps of Uncle Rick's cramped paw."

"Or slashed by my deadly claws," growled Uncle Rick. "I've got those too, same as anyone else."

Mom ignored him.

"So it is with lowered ears and a drooping tail that I inform you all that this is the last day we will ever spend with our lovable though embarrassingly furless mascot," she said with a quivering sigh.

"Whew," exhaled Aunt Trudy. "That's a relief. I was bracing myself for bad news. I thought you were going to adopt him or something."

"I knew we were fattening him up for a reason," Grampa barked eagerly, licking his saggy lips. "Who gets to kill him? My jaws aren't what they used to be, and I don't have much spring in my step. Somebody, please save me some gristle."

Mom didn't pay Grampa any mind.

"Nobody's killing my little Pig Face," she said, growling firmly. "After so much time has gone by, it would be like killing one of our own, which is something we never do, outside of a battle with Dad. No, we won't be savagely ripping off his head and then feasting ravenously on his warm, bloody guts. Instead, we will be dropping him off to fend for himself at the far edge of the woods. There's a moose trail near there that Dad and I would like to check out. With any luck, we'll bring down a young bull and gorge on fresh meat till our stomachs explode."

"Hooray!" cried Aunt Trudy and Uncle Rick and Grampa.

Callum had been attending to all this with mixed feelings. On the one hand, he was glad that Dad and Aunt Trudy and Uncle Rick and Grampa weren't going to rip off his head and feast ravenously on his warm, bloody guts. On the other, it made him sad to think of leaving the den, and he was anxious, too, about being dropped off to fend for himself at the far edge of the woods. And he hated the thought of missing out on the moose dinner, if it happened.

But he knew that Mom had always looked after him, one way or another, in between licking the skin off his cheek. If she thought that the far edge of the woods was the place for him to be, then he could do worse than check it out.

I'm *fierce,* he reminded himself as he always did in times of stress and tension. I'm *savage.* I am a *wild thing*!

"So that's that," growled Dad. "We're off to hunt up some moose. And we're stopping by the far edge of the woods on the way."

Whereupon the whole pack filed out of the den, with Callum bringing up the rear as he usually did, crawling on his hands and knees on the ground, which was as hard, frozen, and rocky as ever.

CHAPTER THREE

Callum at the Train Station

From the bluff at the far edge of the woods, Callum could see an enormous den in the distance, made out of straight strips of tree and smooth slabs of stone. Even from far away, it looked very impressive.

And he could see a lot of other animals like him down there, all walking on their hind legs. The others of his species were mostly taller and fatter than he was. It was sort of intimidating. He could feel an Omega moment coming on.

"That's it," snarled Dad. "This is as far as we go. Ugh! I can barely stand the stench, even from here. It makes me sick."

"I feel faint," complained Aunt Trudy.

"So do I," griped Uncle Rick. "I'm totally dizzy."

Mom licked Callum's cheek for what must have been the ten-millionth time. "I'm going to miss my Salty Lollipop," she whimpered.

"Tie me up with squirrel tails and spank me with a toad-stool!" barked Grampa. "What are we doing, loitering like this halfway out in the open? I'm too slow for target practice!"

"We're out of here," snarled Dad and turned back to the cover of the forest.

"Finally," complained Aunt Trudy.

"Moose ahoy!" said Uncle Rick.

"Good-bye, my little Pig Face," said Mom. And then she howled. And without even thinking about it, Callum howled back. And from within the forest, Dad and Aunt Trudy and Uncle Rick and Grampa all started howling too.

It wasn't surprising. Howling was that contagious.

All of the other animals like Callum at the enormous den in the distance stopped what they were doing and stared in their direction in shock.

"Oops," Mom said, "you know what to do, my little Pig Face. Good-bye."

And when Callum looked again, she was gone.

For the first time that he could remember, he was alone in the woods.

There was no one to share a den with, or a bite of spleen.

The wind made a whistling sound as it passed through the evergreen boughs overhead. It sounded lonely.

A lone hawk screeched as it circled the cloudy sky.

It sounded hungry.

Mom was right, as usual. Callum knew what to do. He hiked past the clearing, waded through a stream, clambered down a bluff, trudged along a gulley, climbed over a fence, walked across a field, jumped over a ditch, crossed a road, and finally ended up at the enormous den that he had seen in the distance.

It was even more impressive up close. Instead of random rocks, there were steps leading to higher levels. Tall, covered walls kept out the wind and snow, with helpful spaces to see through to search for prey. And there were smooth, flat things to sit on instead of the bumpy ground.

The place was practically jammed with upright creatures like him, all rushing to and fro like absolute maniacs. They didn't seem to be running *away* from something, but *toward* something instead. Whatever it was, they were in an awful hurry to catch up with it.

Oops!

Somebody bumped into him.

Hey!

Somebody else bumped into him.

I'm *fierce*, Callum reminded himself. I'm *savage.* I am a *wild thing*!

He bared his teeth, made his hands look like deadly claws, and growled for all he was worth. After that, the other animals looked at him like he was crazy, but they stayed far enough away from him that nobody bumped into him again.

This aggressive behavior used up his last ounce of strength, however. It wasn't surprising. He'd been trudging through the forest since dawn.

I'll just take a little nap, he decided. Then I'll figure out what I'm going to do next.

He climbed onto an empty bench and before he knew it, he was fast asleep.

As tired as he was, he had a great dream.

He was crouching in the deep woods, his sensitive nose tingling with the sharp scent of freshly snapped evergreen boughs.

Up ahead, a mighty bull moose crashed through the brush, obliterating all that stood in its path with the thunderous onslaught of its powerful hooves.

He raced to catch up with it, running on all fours like a born quadruped.

Dad, a few lengths behind him, shouted encouragement. "Cut it off at the pass, son!" he instructed.

Callum sprang forward. With a few energetic leaps and bounds he was nose-to-nose with the rampaging ruminant.

Lunging savagely, he locked his jaws around the massive animal's thickly bearded neck. The furious beast reared up angrily, swinging him a full ten feet off the ground. Still he kept his jaws clamped tightly, and even increased his grip a notch or two.

With an awful suddenness his steely incisors broke through the moose's thick beard and tough hide. A shower of hot blood sprayed in every direction, and about a gallon of it flowed directly into his open mouth and down his greedy throat.

By this time, Dad had caught up with the prey and was mercilessly raking its unprotected flanks with his deadly claws. Mom, Aunt Trudy, and Uncle Rick soon joined in, doing all they could to bring the mammoth mammal to its knees.

The moose aimed a kick at Aunt Trudy's head. Quick as a flash, Callum dashed to her side, lowered his fearsome jaws, and snapped its leg in two just before its heavy hoof could connect with the sore spot between her eyes.

With one last awful groan, the beleaguered beast fell to the ground, rolled over, bellowed a death cry, and then kicked the bucket.

The pack stood in awed anticipation of the enormous feast before them. There was more food on the table than anyone could remember, even Grampa, and he had seen some prodigious pig-outs in the glorious days of yore.

"I've never seen so much food before in all my life," marveled Mom, her yellow eyes shining. "And to think, we owe it all to my little Pig Face!"

"Well done, son," said Dad. "I couldn't be more proud of you. You never have to roll on your back to me again. Uncle Rick, though, had better brush up on his technique."

"One lousy moose, and the kid gets Beta status?" griped Uncle Rick.

"You'd better watch your back, Ricky," said Grampa. "I might just decide to challenge you next."

"Oh Great Spirit that guides the Sun and Moon and Lights the Stars and watches over All That Lives in This World and Beyond," Dad said as everyone gathered in respectful silence for grace, "we thank You for this nourishing meal, although You had less to do with it than my adopted son here, who doesn't even have a hint of a tail but was able to bring down this bull moose almost entirely on his own. Like I've always said, there's only room for one Alpha Male in this pack. And I know who's getting the position the minute I step down to Beta."

"Great," sighed Uncle Rick. "Omega, here I come."

With that, the whole group shot forward, and within a few minutes they cleaned the moose to the bone.

Afterward, they all lay around burping and farting and watched in amazement as Callum picked a stick off the ground and poked it into a hole in an old rotten tree stump nearby. They were even more amazed to see him pull it out covered with greasy, spicy termites. If they could have clapped their paws, they would have applauded.

As stuffed as they were, no one could resist taking a few succulent bites of the peppery bugs.

And then everyone gathered around and happily howled their lungs out at the rising moon, and Callum howled the loudest and wildest of all.

And then . . .

"*What* in the *world* are you *doing*?" came a loud, officious voice that broke through Callum's dream like a wrecking ball.

"*Why* on *earth* are you making a sound like a *broken ambulance siren*? Are you *injured* in some way, perhaps? Or just *touched* in the *head*?"

Callum opened his eyes and squinted in the bright light. Standing over him on the train station platform was a strange older animal with silvery hair, dressed in a long coat of what appeared to be some kind of animal pelt. He could tell from his experience in the Wild that it wasn't real fur. It was something else. It looked every bit as warm as real fur, though.

He couldn't believe his ears. For a confusing moment or two, he wasn't sure if he was still dreaming or not. This strange older animal had made sounds, and the sounds had made *sense*. They weren't merely *noises*. They were *words*.

"Oh, dear," shouted the older animal in alarm. "You *must* have *hit your head*. Do you know where you *are*? You are at the *train station*. This is *America*."

Without really thinking about it, Callum opened his mouth and made words of his own.

"Talking you me to?" he asked numbly, not getting the words in the proper order, which was understandable. He was pretty rusty at it.

"Of *course* I'm talking to *you*. Who *else* would it be?" the strange woman bellowed in reply. For that's what she was, Callum suddenly knew. She wasn't an animal at all, but a woman. And the other animals were people, and he was a person too.

I *am* smart! he thought proudly. And not just with sticks and termites. Future Alpha material, no doubt about it.

You'd think that the most unusual thing about this woman was her furry coat, or her deafening voice. But it was neither of those things. The most unusual thing about her was that she understood what Callum had said, even though he was rusty.

She's talking my language! he realized all of a sudden. The same language my thoughts are made of!

And then he remembered with a jolt of understanding that he had heard words before. Not only that, but he had loved words, once upon a time. He had loved to hear them, and he had loved to speak them. It had something to do with the shadowy figures at the back of his mind—but he didn't want to think about them. He was still mad at them. Furious, really.

"*Really* understand you what said I?" he asked the loud woman, just to make sure. Obviously, he had some work to do, if he wanted his words to come out right. This rediscovered language was trickier to speak than to think!

"I admit, your *foreign accent* is a *little thick*," she allowed dramatically, practically shouting her head off. "I may not grasp the *double meanings,* nor fully comprehend the *finer points.* But as for the *general message,* yes, I *believe* I got the drift. I am Mrs. Throckmorton-Gordon. *Who* are *you?*"

"Mrs. *huh?*" said Callum, who had never heard such a long name in his life, as far as he could recall, let alone so many challenging words.

"You may call me Mrs. T-G," said the strange woman considerately. She had obviously run into this problem before.

"Mrs. T-G," Callum repeated carefully.

"That's right," she replied approvingly, as if he had passed some sort of test. "*What* shall I call *you?*"

"Er . . . Clam," Callum said automatically. "My name is Clam."

The answer just popped into his head. It was something he dimly recalled having said before, something someone had taught him to say . . . but who? The shadowy figures at the back of his mind? He didn't want to think about them.

"*Speak up,*" insisted Mrs. T-G in a verbal blast of noise that nearly knocked him over. "I am somewhat hard of hearing, owing to an *unfortunate accident* in my *youth,* when I was *pulled* aboard a *moving hay cart* by my *ears.* The problem comes and goes. Sometimes I can hear a *pin drop.* Other times I can't hear a *thing.* What did you say your name is, again?"

"*My name is Clam,*" Callum said loudly. (Of course, his real name was Callum. He hadn't remembered it right.)

"My word!" exclaimed Mrs. T-G. "You were named after a mollusk! Now I've heard *everything*! I'm glad to meet you, Clam."

With that, she slapped him heartily on the back.

Callum was thunderstruck. This loud, tiny woman was even more of an Alpha Female than Mom. Instinctively he rolled over onto his back, exposing his vulnerable throat and underside.

"*Good heavens!*" cried Mrs. T-G in alarm. "What on *earth* are you doing *now*? This is a train station! There is only *one reason* I can think of why a person would crawl on this germy floor, and that is because he has *lost* or *misplaced* his *fare*. Is that the case with you? *Do* stand up and behave properly."

"Me no lost fare my," said Callum, getting up and brushing himself off. "I no have fare. What is fare?"

Honestly, he thought, this is getting embarrassing. That sounded terrible. I've really got to get the hang of speaking the same way I'm thinking!

Mrs. T-G was more accepting of his bad grammar than he was, however.

"What is fair, indeed?" she replied philosophically, looking off into the distance. "That is an excellent question, Clam. It seems to me that there is very little sense to what is fair and unfair in this world. I've always thought it was extremely unfair that I was pulled aboard the moving hay cart by my ears. I shall never forget that terrible day. Never allow anyone to use your ears as a handle or grip."

"Yes, Mrs. T-G," Callum replied automatically and then thought excitedly, I have a name! My name is Clam, like the mollusk! It struck him as a wonderful thing. He had never heard of a mollusk before, but it sounded important. If it were an animal, it was probably even higher than wolves on the food chain. Of course, it wouldn't have been surprising if he had forgotten his name altogether, considering that for the past few years Mom had only ever called him "Pig Face" and "Salty Lollipop," and Grampa called him "Fire-head."

"Stand up straight and let me get a good look at you," Mrs. T-G commanded, and Callum obediently did as she asked.

She eyed the strange markings sewn onto his navy blue blazer.

"Hmmm. You attend the Hargrove Academy for the Gifted, Bright, and Perceptive Child, I see," she remarked agreeably. "You must be a foreign exchange student. Please, don't tell me what country you're from. I won't even guess. It's all one world to me, and we are all one people. It is our sacred mission in life to link arms and march hand in hand bravely together into the future. Tsk, tsk. I don't know what our school system is coming to when it allows students to run amok like wild animals. Your hair is a tangled mess, your dirty hands are a disgrace, but I am glad to see that you keep your face immaculately clean."

For once, Callum was grateful for Mom's bristly tongue, which could strip the bark off an oak tree.

"As it happens," said Mrs. T-G, "I am traveling to the city today and I can spare you a punch on my fare card. You may repay me whenever you like. *Wait . . .*"

All at once she stopped dead in her tracks and stared at Callum's head in amazement, as if seeing it for the very first time.

"Your *hair* . . . ," she said quietly, sounding as though she were speaking from somewhere far, far away.

"Your hair?" Callum repeated, confused.

"No," corrected Mrs. T-G. "Not *my* hair—*your* hair."

"*My* hair," Callum repeated.

"*Exactly*," said Mrs. T-G, all in a daze. "That beautiful shade of bright red makes me feel happy . . . and yet it makes me feel sad. It makes me elated, but also deflated. Seeing it, I want to sing and dance and cry my eyes out at the same time. No. That's not it. I want to fly a kite and then crawl into bed and pull the covers over my head simultaneously. Yes. That's more like what I mean."

Oh, no, thought Callum in alarm. Something was wrong with Mrs. T-G. She was sounding as nutty as Aunt Trudy after being kicked in the head by a caribou. He decided to do what Dad always did with Aunt Trudy. He narrowed his eyes and growled at her for all he was worth.

It did the trick, thank goodness.

"Oh, my!" she said abruptly, snapping out of her trance. "What were we talking about?"

"My hair," Callum replied with relief.

"Oh, yes. Your hair . . . ," said Mrs. T-G, who then studied it even more closely, ". . . is *absolutely filthy.* I cannot *possibly* travel with anyone who resembles a *tumbleweed.* You must come with me to the barber to make yourself presentable

[35]

before the train arrives. Or would you prefer to wait around to see if any better benefactor happens to show up out of the blue to help you out?"

"I go with you," Callum said without any hesitation. "Mrs. T-G big Alpha Female."

"*I beg your pardon?*" exclaimed Mrs. T-G, shouting again. "I'm sure I didn't hear you properly. Mind my damaged ears, if you please."

"*What be barber?*" Callum shouted back, then thought, darn it, that wasn't right either.

In way of reply, Mrs. T-G stuck out her hand. Callum took it, and she marched him directly to the opposite end of the platform, where a striped pole stood beside a door where some painted words said DENNIS O'MALLEY, BARBER. MEN'S HAIR, WOMEN'S HAIR, CHILDREN HALF OFF.

Of course, Callum couldn't read any of that. But there were pictures there as well, and he could see that a barber had something to do with ripping the hair off people's heads.

He didn't like that one bit. But when he tried to let go of Mrs. T-G's hand, she gripped his hand harder!

CHAPTER FOUR

Meanwhile, at a School in the City . . .

At the same time Callum was dreading meeting someone who ripped the hair off people's heads, a girl at a school in the city was dealing with something that made her want to pull out her own bright red hair in frustration.

She was jotting down some classwork in her notebook and trying to concentrate, but the boy seated in the desk behind her kept rudely kicking her chair. His name was Billy Bankson, and he was goofing off with his friends before the final bell rang for class.

In point of fact, it wasn't a bell that announced the beginning of class, but four musical notes played on a xylophone broadcasted over the PA system. That may sound unusual, but the school itself was unusual. It was called the Hargrove Academy for the Gifted, Bright, and Perceptive Child, and it had produced some of the finest minds in the country.

The redheaded girl was doing her best to put her giftedness, brightness, and perceptiveness to work, but it wasn't easy with all the kicking going on.

"Attention, everybody," Billy said loudly, addressing the entire class and still kicking away. "I want everyone to know that Jose stole my rucksack at the lodge yesterday."

"For the last time, I did not steal your rucksack," objected Jose Alvarez, who was one of Billy's friends, although you wouldn't know it by the way Billy treated him. Billy was always putting Jose in the doghouse for no good reason whatsoever.

"For the last time, I know you did," said Billy. "And you took all my clothes that were in it. That better not be my blazer you're wearing today. And you better not be wearing my Spidey undies, either."

"As if," scoffed Jose. "I don't even like Spiderman. Batman is so much cooler."

"Give me your Whing Dings," Billy commanded. Whing Dings were his favorite sugary junk food, and Jose always had a package or two in his rucksack.

"I don't see why I should," said Jose, but it was a pointless objection. His Whing Dings were history.

"Do you have to be such a pain?" said a bright-eyed girl sitting at a desk in the front row, turning around and looking at Billy severely. "You're always causing a disruption. Some of us are trying to get our act together and prepare for class."

"You're always so perfect, Becca Adams," said Billy mockingly. "One day you might wake up and find that you've wasted your whole life being perfectly stupid."

The redheaded girl looked up from her notebook with concern. She and Becca were best friends. Billy was a master of insults, and that one was especially hurtful. Becca prided herself on the fact that she wasn't anywhere close to being stupid. She was one of the brightest kids in school.

She gave Becca a look of heartfelt commiseration, but Becca didn't need it, fortunately. Although she was shocked as well, Becca rose above Billy's bullying taunt and refused to let it hurt her feelings. She merely rolled her eyes and went back to studying.

Ding-dong, ding-dong went the xylophone over the PA, and the life sciences teacher entered the room. His name was Mr. Sears, and the class fell silent, even Billy. Mr. Sears didn't tolerate nonsense from anyone.

"Settle down, everybody," he said. "I want to start things off today by going over your assignment for next week. First of all, in preparation for the report you're going to write, I want you all to take a moment to imagine what it would be like to live among a group of animals in the Wild. Whether you choose to live in a herd, a flock, or a pack, I want you to answer four important questions. What kind of food do you eat, and where do you get it? Where do you sleep? And what role do you play in the group?"

The class took a few minutes to think. Almost everyone participated. (Billy only pretended to.)

"It's not easy being a wild animal, is it?" asked Mr. Sears afterward. "Now, imagine that your species is endangered, and it's just gotten ten times harder for you to survive. You could use a little help, don't you think? Humans have got so big a say in what happens on this planet that I think we should view it as our duty to look out for our fellow creatures whenever we can. With that in mind, I'm handing out a list of endangered species. Your assignment is to choose two of these animal groups and outline a plan to assist them in some way in five hundred words or more."

He went around the room, giving everyone a list, and every student took it eagerly, except for Billy Bankson, who accepted it like it was a death sentence.

When she saw how long the list was, the redheaded girl's heart sank. There were too many endangered species to count. She wanted to help them all, but what could she do, with her limited resources? She suddenly felt very small and inconsequential. She didn't often feel that way, and didn't like it one bit.

Her family hadn't been camping in years, but she'd always sensed a close connection to the Wild. Whether she was in the classroom or her bedroom at home or on the city street, there were times when she could practically smell the pine trees in the woods and the rich, tangy scent of forest soil.

After thinking it over, she chose the two species that were geographically farthest away from her. She figured that they needed her help the most. But more than help them, she wanted to *comfort* them somehow. The closest way to describe it is that she wanted to give them a hug. But that was ridiculous, wasn't it? You couldn't hug a polar bear.

"Now that you've had a little while to look the list over, has anyone chosen their species yet?" asked Mr. Sears.

"I have," replied a shy, pudgy boy wearing glasses that looked much too big for his head. His name was Tito Jones.

"Yes, Tito," said Mr. Sears. "And what might they be?"

"I can't pronounce the Latin names, but I've picked elkhorn coral and Adler's Mottled Treefrog," answered Tito. "Elkhorn coral are important reef-builders, and they are threatened by pollution. Adler's Mottled Treefrog lives in Mexico. It's threatened by loss of habitat."

"Lila, what about you?" asked Mr. Sears, turning to the redheaded girl. "What species do you plan to write about? Do you know yet?"

"Yes. I plan to help *Ursus maritimus,* the polar bears, and *Eudyptes sclateri,* the Erect-crested penguins," answered the redheaded girl with conviction, whose name was indeed Lila. "The polar bears in particular. The Arctic ice caps are melting earlier than ever, but they need ice caps in order to hunt for seals, which is their primary food group. Without seals to eat, they're going to go hungry. And I'm so very sorry about that."

It suddenly struck her that what she had said sounded a lot like an apology. Why should she apologize? It wasn't like she was personally responsible for the animals' struggles in the barren wilderness.

"All right, everybody," said Mr. Sears in a satisfied tone. "It sounds as if you're all off to a rousing start. Now let's continue with our oceanography studies. Everyone take out your textbooks and turn to chapter five."

The class carried on studying from chapter five, but Lila was distracted and paid no attention for once. Billy kicked her chair again, but she didn't care about that anymore. Thoughts of polar bears and penguins and a dozen other endangered species ran through her mind, and she wracked her brains for solutions to their problems. For although there were a few human beings so irritating that she would be happy to put them out of their misery, she believed all animals deserved protecting. She could imagine what it felt like to be lost and alone and in need of help, although she had never really experienced it herself. She was going to help the polar bears and penguins if it was the last thing she did. She felt she knew exactly what they needed, and what they wanted, as if she were there in the wilderness with them, side by side. You might say that, after her last camping trip to the woods years ago, she had left a part of herself in the Wild.

CHAPTER FIVE

Callum, Fit to Travel

Mr. O'Malley's barbershop at the train station smelled both sharp and sweet inside. (It was a mixture of rubbing alcohol and orange-blossom cologne.) Callum had never whiffed anything as intriguing as that before. It almost made him forget how afraid he was of having the hair pulled out of his head.

The shop contained two shiny silver chairs, and Mr. O'Malley was seated in one of them with his nose buried in what Callum later learned was a newspaper. He was pretty hairy for a barber. He sported curly gray hair that grew past his shoulders and a bushy gray beard. A little bell on the wall jangled merrily when the door opened, and he looked up from the paper.

"Well, well," he said with a grin, probably. It was hard to tell what was going on exactly under all that hair. "If it isn't Mrs. T-G. What can I do you for today? A trim? A waxing?

A paraffin dip for your poor tired hands? Perhaps we can shave that furry coat of yours a little."

"My hair is a perfect length at present, Mr. O'Malley," said Mrs. T-G politely. "And so is my coat. And my hands are neither poor nor tired today, but at least *one* of them is not exactly clean. Please bring me a small cloth soaked in disinfectant so I can sanitize the one I mean, which has recently been soiled by contact with an *unbelievably* dirty hand."

This Mr. O'Malley did as she asked without any delay. She thoroughly wiped both her hands and then passed the cloth to Callum. "Your turn, Clam," she said firmly. "Remove that grime forthwith, and make a good show of it, please."

Callum took the cold, wet cloth and copied her actions exactly. The cloth was white to begin with, but it was far from that when he returned it to Mr. O'Malley.

"Very good," said Mrs. T-G contentedly when he was finished. "And now, Mr. O'Malley, I would like you to direct your professional attentions to my young friend Clam here. He is a foreign exchange student at the Hargrove Academy, and it seems he has been using his *head* as a *dust mop* for some unknown reason."

"Clam, is it? Like the mollusk? Well, I never!" said Mr. O'Malley, squinting in Callum's direction. He fetched a pair of wiry spectacles from his apron pocket and strapped them in place. "Yes, a very serious misuse of the old noggin spaghetti," he announced after a thorough examination.

"The hair on your head is meant for adornment, young man. Not for sweeping, scouring, or polishing when you don't have a broom or a cleaning pad handy. Sit in this chair, and I'll see what I can do to tame this wild tangle. If you will be so kind, Mrs. T-G, you may take a seat by the window. You'll find a new issue of *Vegetable Treats* on the table to pass the time."

"Don't mind if I do," said Mrs. T-G. She plopped herself down in a comfortable chair by the window and then picked up a magazine filled with glossy color photos of various garden vegetables, all ripe and juicy.

"How is your garden at home coming along, Mrs. T-G?" Mr. O'Malley inquired, but she was too fascinated by a full-page color photo of a well-scrubbed carrot to pay any attention. She was practically chewing it to pieces with her eyes.

"I've been having a difficult time with my rose bushes," Mr. O'Malley went on, not that she noticed. "Infested with aphids, all of them. I had no choice but to chop every last one of my plants down to the ground. Chop, chop, chop!"

He picked up a gleaming pair of scissors and approached Callum's head with them.

"Just leave a little on the top, Mr. O'Malley, if you will be so kind," instructed Mrs. T-G. "And prune it up above his ears."

"Chop, chop, chop!" Mr. O'Malley said again. "If you ask me, that's the only thing to do when a plant's been infested with bugs."

Snip!

With one fell swoop of his scissors he put a considerable dent in Callum's hair helmet.

Plonk!

The scissors hit something hard.

"Bless me," said Mr. O'Malley. "Was that a *twig* in your hair?"

Ker-*chonk!*

The scissors hit something harder than a twig.

"Mercy!" cried Mr. O'Malley. "Was that a *rock*? I've heard of hair that's hard to cut, but this is ridiculous!"

"We don't have all day," Mrs. T-G said firmly. "The train to the city is due any minute. Simply take out your sturdiest shaver and *shear* him like a *sheep*. My, what beautiful spears of asparagus!"

She looked at the magazine photo of asparagus as if she had fallen in love with it.

Mr. O'Malley had in fact worked as a farmer in his younger days, and he had sheared countless sheep in his time. He reached into a drawer, pulled out a heavy-duty metal shaver, plugged it in, and set about removing the dirty, matted fleece from Callum's head.

"*Great Scott!*" he exclaimed after two or three strokes of the shears. "This scalp is *infested* with *lice*."

"Dear oh dear," Mrs. T-G said to Callum calmly. "You *do* need cleaning up, don't you?"

"What be lice?" Callum asked interestedly.

"Lice be—I mean, lice *are* bloodsucking parasites that live among the hair follicles on people's heads whenever they get the opportunity," said Mr. O'Malley. "They're nasty little bugs. Despicable pests. Like aphids, only worse." He wiggled his hands in a buglike way and made an evil, creepy face, to show what he meant. "And they are extremely easy to pass from one person to another, so if you don't mind, I'm going to put on a pair of rubber gloves before we proceed any further. I see you're looking at a rutabaga," he said, craning his neck in Mrs. T-G's direction, where a glossy picture of the vegetable cross between a cabbage and a turnip could be seen in the magazine she was holding. "I boiled a rutabaga for dinner the other night. My goodness, did it taste good!"

"Do lice taste good?" asked Callum, who was feeling rather hungry by this time. He had eaten plenty of bugs before, and it had been a long while since his last bite of gristle.

"Do *lice* taste good?" echoed Mr. O'Malley, taken aback. Although he found the question disgusting, he was willing to consider the possibility. "I wouldn't think so. But then I've never tried any. I'd stick to a nice ham on rye sandwich instead. Or, if I were serving the lady, a cucumber and watercress sandwich with a touch of dill."

He winked in Mrs. T-G's direction, but she didn't pay him any mind. A gleaming photo of a beefsteak tomato had just captured her attention.

"Mrs. T-G is a vegetarian," Mr. O'Malley explained fondly to Callum. "Like a caribou or a moose, she only eats what springs forth from the soil."

It was Callum's turn to be taken aback. Of all the unlikely things! Mrs. T-G was a grass eater. It wasn't at all what he expected from such an Alpha Female.

"I do not graze for sustenance," Mrs. T-G corrected Mr. O'Malley sharply. "Nor do I comb the treetops in search of green leaves and tender shoots. I consume a wide variety of foods, minus the meat element, purchased at specialty stores at enormous cost."

"She may sound fierce," Mr. O'Malley confided to Callum with another grin that you could barely see under all his hair, "but make her a nice Waldorf salad and she'll as much as kiss your hand."

Callum grinned back. For a barber who ripped the hair off people's heads, Mr. O'Malley seemed like a really nice guy. But his grin nearly switched to a grimace. He was hearing a lot of new words, and trying to keep up was a pain. It seemed like his brain had never worked harder, and the gears in his mind were starting to wobble.

Mr. O'Malley adjusted his rubber gloves with a snap.

"Now, about those bugs," he said sternly. "You'd be surprised at how common lice are, even at the best schools. Understandably, shame and embarrassment and the fear of being outcast like lepers with cooties keep students from checking their scalps as often as they should. Not to worry. I'm not so weak-minded. I've simply got to sterilize every single piece of equipment in the shop when we're done, which is something that I do around here every day anyway."

He finished cutting Callum's bug-infested hair, then unplugged the electric shaver and wiped it clean. Then he swept up the pile of hair, twigs, and rocks from under Callum's chair with a hand brush and dumped it all in the trash, hand brush included.

Next, he brought out a bucket filled with a soapy, prickly smelling liquid and rapidly and thoroughly mopped the entire floor. Finally he pulled a lever on the chair Callum was sitting in, and the chair tilted back so that Callum's head was poised directly over the sink.

"Now we'll attack them where they live!" Mr. O'Malley said eagerly. "I've got just the stuff to blast those unholy parasites back to where they belong. It may sting a bit, but don't let it worry you. That's how you know it's working. And don't be surprised if your hair comes out a shade or two lighter afterward. That usually happens."

"Careful you don't cause any serious damage," Mrs. T-G said placidly, looking with misty-eyed affection at a photo of a shucked ear of corn. "We don't want any lawsuits or any trips to the hospital. Not if we're going to make our train on time."

"Don't worry about anything happening to me," said Mr. O'Malley. "I've got barber's insurance."

He took a big brown bottle off the shelf, which hissed as he uncapped it. Then he poured its entire contents on Callum's head. Just like he said, it stung, but not a bit—it stung like crazy!

It sure is working, Callum thought nervously. He didn't think he could stand it if it worked any better. But in a minute or two Mr. O'Malley was rinsing it away with vigorous blasts from the hose attachment on the sink faucet.

"Hope that's not too hot," he said, recklessly squirting scalding water all over Callum's face, ears, and neck.

"There you have it!" he declared proudly when he was done. "That's my A-number-one treatment for the eradication of lice. Let's see any blankety-blank louse survive that!"

He vigorously rubbed Callum's wet head with a fluffy white towel, whipped it off with a flourish, and then he caught sight of the results.

"Great Scott!" he cried. "I thought your bright red hair couldn't get any brighter. Live and learn!"

Callum had to take a moment to make sure that *he* had survived. He stared at his newly cropped and brighter red hair in the mirror. At first it was a definite shock to realize that the person staring back at him was himself. No wonder the pack had thought he was so strange, and Grampa had called him Firehead. He didn't look at all like a North American Gray Wolf or Timber Wolf (*Canis lupus*), and his bright red hair resembled a forest fire at sunset. After he had recovered his senses, he was pleased to see how much his ears stuck out now that his hair was chopped off. Dad had always complained that he could never see his ears properly. If only he could see them now. You couldn't miss them.

"That is a considerable turn for the better," said Mrs. T-G and shut her magazine after a final lingering look at a centerfold of Brussels sprouts. "Just in time, too, with exactly one minute to spare. Thank you for your trouble, Mr. O'Malley. You have earned your fee and more. I am including a gratuity that should go a good way toward restocking your supply of disinfectant for the shop."

"You're much too kind, Mrs. T-G," said Mr. O'Malley. "I'm happy to oblige. It was good to meet you, Clam. I like mollusks, and I'm a fan of the Hargrove Academy. Wherever you're from, welcome to America. We're happy to have you."

And with that, he settled into the shiny silver chair again and picked up reading the paper just where he'd left off.

The train was pulling into the station as Mrs. T-G and Callum left the barbershop. There was the ear-splitting shriek of rusty brakes on the tracks and a stinging blast of grit amid the powerful stench of diesel fumes.

"Ah, the romance of train travel!" cried Mrs. T-G eagerly, sucking it all in as much as she could.

Callum tried not to cough his lungs out. He'd only ever breathed the crystal-fresh air of the Wild before. These abrasive pollutants were a shock to his system. He kind of liked the smell of diesel fumes, however. For some strange reason it made him excited. The unknown suddenly seemed sort of fun. He looked forward to this unexpected adventure.

"All aboard who's going aboard," called the porter. "You're just in time, Mrs. Throckmorton-Gordon."

"I always am, Charlie," said Mrs. T-G. "Are my bags safely stowed?"

"I believe they are, ma'am."

"Thank you, Charlie. Then I'll see you inside. Come along, Clam. All aboard who's going aboard most definitely means the two of us."

And she fairly yanked him aboard the train.

There was so much hustle and bustle aboard the train that Callum could hardly keep track. Same as they did at the station, the people there were all rushing to and fro in a frenzy. It was easy to get lost in the shuffle.

"Over here, Clam," said Mrs. T-G, yanking him toward some seats at the rear of the compartment. "You take the window. The light is too bright for someone who desperately needs a midmorning nap. I'll take the aisle, and we can keep the seat between us free. Neutral territory, so to speak. Ah, Charlie. There you are again. Here is my fare card. Please take it with you and have it punched twice, once for me and once for my traveling companion. We're ever so happy to be aboard and safely seated finally. Is there an extra pillow handy? Thank you."

As soon as Charlie moved on, Mrs. T-G withdrew a fabric eyeshade from her bag, slipped it over her head, lay back against her pillow and then fell sound asleep, her mouth drooping open wider than Callum thought possible.

He looked out the window and marveled at the vast expanse of shiny metal tracks.

And then the train began to move, and he felt like screaming his head off.

CHAPTER SIX

Callum on the Train

Callum had never experienced anything like a moving train before. It was almost too much for him.

At first, he was startled by the intense forward motion, then upset, and then he wanted to jump out of his seat and run for his life.

It took all of his willpower simply to remain where he was.

The compartment rocked. The compartment lurched. The compartment swayed back and forth as the train rounded a bend. And he held onto his seat with a grip of steel.

He wondered what Mom and Dad would do in a situation like this. It was a pretty good bet that they would rage up and down the compartment destroying everything in their paths. First of all, they would attack and kill everyone in sight, savagely ripping at their victims' fleshy abdomens so that their guts spilled out all hot and slimy. Then they would claw the furniture to shreds before finally flinging their frantic bodies at the windows until the glass shattered or they beat themselves senseless, whichever came first.

It was not the kind of behavior Callum could really pull off, he thought with regret. Even when he was a part of Mom and Dad's world, he was no match for them when it came to a rampage. And he was a person now.

The view outside the window only served to confirm the fact that he was no longer a child of the Wild. As the woods fell away in the distance, more and more buildings appeared along with other such nonforesty things as cars, billboards, and telephone poles. With every passing minute he felt smaller and lonelier, and his already overloaded mind became more and more crammed with difficult questions.

How was he supposed to get along in a world that he knew nothing about? Whose den could he possibly share, if not Mrs. T-G's? Would anyone save him a bite of spleen and pancreas, as kindly old Grampa had done?

The weird thing about it was that everything in this strange new world seemed kind of familiar to him. Had he dreamed about it? It was a possibility. He was always having crazy dreams in the den, sleeping between Mom and Aunt Trudy. Of course, they were mostly about Dad trying to devour him, but there were plenty of other things too.

He glanced across the empty seat at Mrs. T-G, who was still sleeping soundly behind her fabric eyeshade. A little snoring sound emerged from her open mouth. She seemed blissfully unaware that at any moment he might rip open her stomach and then feast on her hot, slimy guts. But then, there was no real danger of that, because he was still stuck gritting his teeth and rigidly holding on to the arms of his chair.

I'm *fierce*, he reminded himself. I'm *savage*. I am a *wild thing*!

Unbelievably, Mrs. T-G wasn't the only one in the compartment who was oblivious to the danger of being inside a metal box that was hurtling forward at unbelievable speed. Several other passengers were snoozing as well, one or two people were reading the newspaper (like Mr. O'Malley had done), and a few of them were peacefully listening to chaotic noises through funny-looking white earpieces.

Callum began to feel just a tiny bit foolish. Really, he was a very brave person. He'd like to see how any of these other people reacted to Dad waking them up in the middle of the night with cold-blooded murder gleaming in his savage yellow eyes. He had taken that in stride. He could have been calmly reading the paper then too, if he'd had one and knew how to read.

Now he had to be equally cool in the face of fresh danger. Was he up to the challenge? He took a deep breath, then let it out, then took another and let that out too, and gradually it didn't seem so frightening to be trapped inside the rocking, tilting, lurching metal box. There was actually something comforting about it, something he couldn't quite put his finger on. It had something to do with a gentle, soothing tune. What was that called again? Oh, yes. A lullaby . . .

He suddenly realized that, although it was still only morning, he was completely worn out after the long trudge through the woods and the ordeal with Mr. O'Malley and the head lice, and all of a sudden the seat he was sitting in felt awfully comfortable and his head felt extremely heavy and his eyelids felt even heavier than that, and he was just experiencing the blessed relief of dreamland coming fast when he heard a loud, familiar voice in his ear.

"*Now, now!*" scolded Mrs. T-G, who was miraculously fully awake and yelling her head off. "We mustn't waste the best part of the morning chasing unicorns and rainbows in Cloud-Cuckoo Land! I don't know about *you,* but I am *absolutely famished.* I suggest we visit the *dining car* and see if we can scare up some *breakfast.*"

In no time at all she was out of her seat and charging down the aisle.

The idea of breakfast hit Callum like a lightning bolt. Although he hadn't thought about it until now, he realized that it had always been one of his very favorite words. He shot out of his seat as well and caught up with Mrs. T-G just as she was exiting the compartment through the connecting door.

They passed through two more compartments before reaching the dining car, and even before they stepped inside, the intoxicating smells of what he soon learned were eggs, bacon, and hot, buttered toast made Callum so delirious that he thought he was losing his mind.

Before this moment, the most delicious thing he had ever whiffed was the aroma of freshly gutted caribou intestines. Mrs. T-G had no idea about that, of course, but she could plainly see the effect that the smells of the dining-car breakfast were having on him.

"That is the *horrible stench* of *hot grease*," she said matter-of-factly. "You must be a meat eater. Carnivores find the horrible stench of hot grease *practically irresistible*. I pass no judgment on those who choose to *poison* their *bodies* with the rotten and diseased flesh of some *poor, tortured animal.* As for myself, I'm looking forward to something in the way of a simple bran muffin and a nice cup of freshly brewed, fair-trade coffee."

Callum nearly burst with excitement. In his experience, rotten and diseased food always tasted as good as it smelled. He knew he was in for a treat.

As for poor, tortured animals, he had never known a dinner that wasn't tortured at least a little bit before it was devoured. Most dinners were pretty realistic about it and gave up the ghost as soon as the tearing to pieces began. After all, there were only so many links in the food chain. Sooner or later, everyone's number came up. That was Nature's golden rule.

"Here's some pocket lettuce," Mrs. T-G said, pressing a

few crisp, green paper bills in his hand. "Get whatever you feel your conscience will allow. I will save seats for us at a table near the window."

The breakfast was set up cafeteria style. Callum loaded his tray, followed the line to the cashier, and quickly discovered what pocket lettuce was all about. Then he took his tray to the table where Mrs. T-G sat with her bran muffin and steaming cup of coffee and sat down in the seat across from her.

He had helped himself to double portions of bacon and two kinds of sausage. As hungry as he was, though, he didn't dig in right away. First, he lowered his head respectfully.

"Oh Great Spirit that guides the Sun and Moon and Lights the Stars and watches over All That Lives in This World and Beyond," he began, "I thank You for this nourishing meal, although You had less to do with it than Mrs. T-G here, who told me about the dining car in the first place and then gave me the pocket lettuce to trade for the food."

Perhaps it was because he was giving thanks to a higher power, or it could have been because he heard the words especially clearly in his mind; whatever the reason, when he said grace, he got through the whole thing without making a single mistake. He didn't really notice, as he was too caught up in the respectful mood and all. But Mrs. T-G nodded approvingly.

"What an interesting and original way of saying grace

you have in your country," she remarked, greatly touched. "But as for myself, I must decline all responsibility and give full credit to the Great Spirit to which you refer."

"Hey now, there's a boy with an appetite," said a man sitting at a table across from them as Callum gobbled up everything on his plate without pausing to take so much as a single breath. The man looked to be around Mrs. T-G's age and wore a silvery mustache that curled up at the ends.

"Indeed," Mrs. T-G replied sensibly. "That's what comes of a weekend in the Wild at the Hargrove Academy Lodge. It's only to be expected. There is nothing like exposure to the great outdoors to do a body good. After my stay in the National Forest, I myself just might head back for another bran muffin."

"I understand completely," continued the man with the silvery mustache. "Nothing recharges my batteries quite like a weekend at my cabin in the woods. I've been working on it off and on for thirty years now. It's my pride and joy. I wish you could see it."

"Nothing would please me more," said Mrs. T-G warmly. "I spend my weekends working with the Forestry Service to solicit land donations for a new wildlife sanctuary while my husband, Luther, who is a prominent lawyer as well as a former heavyweight boxing champion, takes charge of the legal side back in the city. He has never lost a case in the courtroom or a bout in the ring. My Forestry Service friends and I would be most interested in viewing your property."

"If you'll excuse me," said the man with the silvery mustache, rising from the table abruptly, "I think I'll get another glass of orange juice."

"Did something you say make him go away?" asked Callum between bites of juicy sausage. "A good job you did. I mean . . . you . . . did . . . a . . . good . . . job. It really worked!"

He was concentrating harder now and taking his time in order to speak the words exactly as he heard them in his head, and it was beginning to pay off. But he still had to keep an eye on it and pay strict attention or else the only thing that came out was gobbledygook.

"It isn't polite to talk with your mouth full, Clam," reproved Mrs. T-G. "So *don't*. And anyway, what a ridiculous notion! Why would I want anyone to go away? Everything I said is perfectly true. My husband, Luther, and I are fully committed to helping the Forestry Service create the finest wildlife sanctuary that has ever existed. Luther is in fact a lawyer and has never lost a case. That man was simply not interested in becoming a property donor, I'm afraid. Rest assured the land we are seeking is nowhere near the Hargrove Academy Lodge. The lodge will continue to introduce young people to the magic and charm of the wilderness for many years to come, I trust, even if a few naughty and disagreeable students abuse the privilege. I don't mean you in particular. As a foreign exchange student in unfamiliar territory, you are allowed a little leeway. I'm sure you didn't mean to miss the bus back to school after your weekend away. However, on more than one occasion an unruly Hargrove student by the name of Billy Bankson has joined me on this train. He purposely manages to evade the roll call and causes nothing but trouble. I daresay you know him. He wears a button on his jacket exactly like the one that's pinned to yours."

"Button?" said Callum and looked down to see the badge pinned to his navy blue blazer, with its picture of what appeared to be a little tree growing upside down.

"Yes," affirmed Mrs. T-G, "the peace symbol. I have no reason to suspect that you are not a true believer in worldwide disarmament. But the fact that Billy Bankson wears the peace symbol is just plain wrong, since he is such a bully and so violent. And now let us bus our trays and return to our compartment. As delectable as this breakfast is, I couldn't eat another bite, and I feel another nap coming on strongly."

In another minute Callum was safely back in his seat by the window, and Mrs. T-G was in hers on the aisle, with the empty one between them. Once again she donned her fabric eyeshade and soon fell asleep.

Callum watched the many buildings go by outside the window and wondered what worldwide disarmament meant. If there was one thing he was sure about, it was that he had never heard of *that* before.

With his belly full of rotten and diseased food, he felt a lot stronger than before. He was certain he could meet whatever challenges came his way. It was a good thing too. Whether in the Wild or anywhere else, life was clearly unpredictable. One minute you knew exactly what was what, the next, everything was so uncertain. Just that morning, he had woken up in the crevice in the mountainside. Where would he wake up tomorrow?

CHAPTER SEVEN
Lila at Home

Bright and early, the alarm clock went off in Lila's bedroom in the city.

It didn't wake her because she wasn't asleep. She'd spent the whole night in bed thinking. So when it beeped in its horrible harsh way, instead of freaking out and jumping out of her skin like she usually did when she was rudely awakened from the peaceful depths of silent slumber, she simply rolled over and calmly switched it off and then got out of bed.

"I don't believe it, honey. You're early this morning for once," said her mom when Lila sat down at the breakfast table, washed, brushed, and dressed in her school uniform. "How about some scrambled eggs with your seven-grain toast this morning?"

"I don't eat eggs, Mom, remember?" Lila replied. "I'm a vegan."

"Yes, I know, sweetheart," said her mom. "I haven't

forgotten. They just smell so good that I thought I would share. I'll cut you some slices of apple instead."

"I'd like some granola, please," said Lila. "With rice milk."

"Coming right up," said her mom with a smile. The granola was full of wholesome nuts, and the rice milk was calcium fortified. She liked to see Lila have something nutritious.

"Thanks, Mom," said Lila, digging in.

"Good morning, dear," said Lila's dad to her mom, entering the kitchen intent on straightening his tie. Then he noticed Lila. "Oh, my goodness. Good morning to you too, sweetie. Am I late, or are you early?"

"Good morning, Dad," said Lila absently, chewing her granola thirty-two times for proper digestion. "I'm early."

"Thank goodness," said her dad. "I hate to be late at the art gallery. Those scrambled eggs smell absolutely delicious."

"They do, don't they?" said Lila's mom. "But it's just a refrigerated, pasteurized egg product, dear. Cholesterol free, fat free, and low calorie."

"Just what the doctor ordered," said Lila's dad cheerfully. "At this rate, we'll all live to be a hundred."

"How can you be so insensitive?" demanded Lila sharply, dropping her spoon in her cereal bowl with a clatter.

"Heavens, Lila, what on earth do you mean?" asked her mom, shocked to the core.

"Yes, sweetie, what's gotten into you?" asked her dad, shocked as well.

"The ice packs on the polar caps are melting," said Lila, holding her head in her hands. "And if we don't figure out some way to help them, the polar bears and the penguins will be doomed to extinction!"

"Good gracious," said her dad, sounding relieved that the problem was with the polar bears and the penguins and nothing was wrong with his daughter. "Is it as serious as all that?"

"Don't give up hope, honey," said her mom, sounding relieved as well. "I'm sure the top scientists in the world are working hard at achieving a solution to that."

"But they're *not*!" cried Lila in a fit of temper. "*No one* is doing *anything*!"

"Lila!" her mom reprimanded. "Keep your voice down at the table, please. It's a house rule."

"Sorry," said Lila politely.

"Tell you what," said her dad. "When I get home from the gallery tonight, we'll go online and see what the top scientists in the world are doing to help out with that problem. There might have been a breakthrough or a proposed plan of action. You never know."

Lila brightened at the thought of a breakthrough or a proposed plan of action. She was a little embarrassed about losing her temper. But it was no surprise, really. Lack of sleep always made her cranky.

"It's just that the polar bears and the penguins are in terrible trouble, and something has to be done to help them," she said. "And no one seems to care."

"I care," said her mom.

"So do I," said her dad. "That makes three of us. And that's a really good start. Successful revolutions have been started with less."

"I'd like half a banana, please," said Lila, who felt a little better now. "Thank you."

"Good girl," said her mom, who was always glad when Lila got her potassium.

"So what's on our agendas for today, other than worrying about the polar bears and the penguins?" asked her dad.

"Work at the Science Academy, as usual," replied her mom.

"School at the Hargrove Academy for the Gifted, Bright, and Perceptive Child, as usual," said Lila.

"Work for me too, at the Metropolitan Art Gallery, as usual," said her dad. "Let's rendezvous again here around six o'clock tonight, and we'll touch base at dinner. Have a wonderful and productive day, everyone!"

Lila rinsed her spoon, bowl, and juice glass and put them into the dishwasher, and then went upstairs, brushed her teeth, and packed her rolling tote bag for school. She gathered together the photos of polar bears and penguins that she had printed out from the Internet the night before and placed them in a somber black folder.

She hoped it was true that they weren't necessarily doomed. Maybe they were only going through a rough patch and would come out of it okay.

Lila's own family had gone through a rough patch. Years

ago, her twin brother was lost in the Wild and never found, and her parents had felt so bad about it that they went through a patch so rough that it threatened to ruin their lives.

Lila had been young enough that her grief, though intense at first, had passed relatively quickly, but her parents' remorse about accidentally leaving their only son behind on the family camping trip in the woods had lasted so long that for weeks at a time they had sat around the house all day eating ice cream straight out of the container and watching TV.

In the beginning, they had pigged out on pricey triple chunk and strawberry swirl while watching Animal Planet and the History channel, but after spending so much time away from their jobs, the day soon came when they could no longer afford expensive ice cream or the cable bill. After that, it was cheap, artificially flavored Neapolitan ice milk and *The Price Is Right* reruns on the regular broadcast channel.

The whole family probably would have been kicked out of the house for failure to pay the mortgage if Lila's Aunt Donaldina and Uncle Luther hadn't stepped in to save the day.

"You've got to snap out of it," Aunt Donaldina told them firmly, to show how much she cared. "You didn't mean to leave that poor boy behind at that campsite, and you have done absolutely everything that is humanly possible to find him. The time has now come to put the whole sorry episode out of your mind and never think of it again, no matter what. That's what I'm going to do."

"Same here," agreed Uncle Luther.

"We'll try," said Lila's mom and dad bravely.

"Then the *subject* is *closed*!" decreed Aunt Donaldina.

Gradually, as time went on, the grieving parents started eating less Neapolitan and watching fewer game shows, and in due course they were back at their jobs and acting pretty much like their usual selves again.

Every now and then, however, something came along to remind them of their loss, and it would send them right back to the frozen dessert section at the grocery store. There was the police investigation, for example, and the lady from Social Services who felt that if they were so thoughtless as to lose one child, they might be expected to lose another. She wanted to take Lila away to live in a family where the parents weren't so absentminded.

But Uncle Luther, who was a lawyer as well as a former heavyweight boxing champion, once again saved the day by representing them in court and convincing the judge to issue a cease and desist order against the lady from Social Services, which stopped her from interfering in their lives ever again. (It was an unqualified victory for Uncle Luther, but he wasn't surprised because he had never lost a case.)

Yes, Lila and her parents had been through a terrible ordeal, but there was nothing to do about it except to move on and try to make every new day a pleasant and rewarding experience, which they did. And now they had a happy home once again. Hopefully, it would work out the same way for the polar bears and the penguins. Certainly, if the ice caps *did* melt away, the polar bears would be worse off than the penguins. Many of them would drown in the rising water, especially the lazy ones and the sick, and then many of those that managed to remain on land would starve to death in a racking and horrible manner, particularly the very young ones and the very old, but the ones that were left after that would have to pick themselves up and face the challenge of adapting to a whole new set of circumstances with a smile and a can-do attitude.

Concerned people like Lila and her parents could still help them out, of course. Care packages of food and nesting materials could be dropped out of airplanes at convenient locations for them, for example, and some big blocks of ice, like the kind that you find at the local convenience store, would offer the poor suffering creatures some temporary relief from the sun's scorching rays.

With any luck, the polar bears and the penguins would eventually reach the point where they looked back on their former life in a wintry wonderland the same way that Lila looked back on once having had a twin brother, which she now viewed as an interesting fact but something that had very little to do with her mostly fun and always interesting life these days.

If that were to be the case with the polar bears and the penguins, she realized, then the five-hundred-word report she was writing for life sciences that was due at the end of the week was going to be a lot more optimistic than she had originally supposed it would be.

She decided to use some of the happier pictures that she had printed late last night, the ones where the polar bears appeared to be smiling and the penguins looked especially playful. It's not that she was ignoring the cold, hard facts. But even endangered animals couldn't be miserable *all* of the time. There was always something to be thankful for, even if it seemed like a teensy-weensy speck compared to a mountain of troubles.

"Bye, now," said Lila's dad, heading off to the art gallery.

"Bye, now," said her mom, heading off to the Science Academy.

"Bye," said Lila, setting out with her rolling tote bag to catch the cab to school, which stopped at the corner three blocks away.

"Coo, coo, coo," called the filthy old pigeons perched on the roofs of the buildings.

"Meow, meow, meow," croaked the mangy tiger cat that lived by the stinky trash cans on the corner.

"Hi, hi, hi," said old Mrs. Hincklemeyer with her rubber gloves and soapy brush, scrubbing her front steps like crazy, same as she did every morning. "Off to school now, Lila? That's nice. Study hard now, you hear? You don't want to end up like me, with nothing else to do but scrub my steps all day."

The sun was shining and the air smelled fresh, except

for around those stinky trash cans. As usual, the big noisy dog in the yard between the two houses down the street barked his head off as Lila passed. And as usual, it made her jump nearly out of her skin.

"Shut up, Ranger, will ya?" yelled a harsh voice from inside the house behind the fence. "If you don't zip your trap, I'm gonna clobber you, ya dumb mutt!"

And then there was the sound of something smashing.

If anything was going to go extinct, Lila wished it would be Ranger. His home life was less than ideal, but as hard as she tried, she simply couldn't feel sorry for him.

Either she was early, or the cab for school was late. It was probably a bit of both. She waited at the corner with Stanley Kramer, who was always the first to show up.

Stanley was a year below Lila at the Hargrove Academy, in the Blue Level. He had shiny black hair at the sides of his head and probably on the top of it too, but she had never seen that side of him because Stanley towered over her like a giant. His navy blue blazer was two sizes too small, and he always smelled like tuna fish and onions, but in a good sort of way, kind of.

Stanley had a knack for growing plants. Although he was still only an amateur botanist, he had already developed a new kind of artichoke that grew as a tree. An important man from the Department of Agriculture had recently contacted him and his parents to offer Stanley a high-paying job in the government when he graduated from Hargrove, with special benefits, such as the use of the president's own private jet. The Kramers were mulling it over in anticipation of better offers from the private sector.

It was nothing to brag about, really, for a student at the Hargrove Academy. All the students there were capable of greatness.

Stanley fairly worshipped everyone in the Yellow Level, and he considered it an honor and a privilege to wait for the cab every morning with Lila.

"Hi, Stanley," she said like she did every morning, and as usual he blushed so deeply that his pudgy cheeks glowed like stoplights.

Then he stammered, "How's your r-r-report coming along?"

Stanley knew all about Lila's life sciences assignment. He made it a point to know everything that went on in the Yellow Level.

"Actually, I've changed my point of view," Lila replied. "Instead of being really fatalistic about it, I've decided to be a little more optimistic where the polar bears and the penguins are concerned."

"W-w-wow," stammered Stanley. His already high opinion of Yellow Level students soared to new heights.

"After all, endangered animals aren't so very different from the rest of us," Lila went on. "Bad things happen to everyone, and we've just got to take whatever comes along and make the best of it. I'm not saying that we shouldn't do our best to make the world a happier and healthier place. But we should look to the future with hope, not despair. We've all got the power to make a change for the better, like you're already doing with your artichoke tree."

"Th-th-thanks," said Stanley, blushing again.

"Still, it's pretty certain that the polar bears and the penguins will need a lot of help in the way of care packages made up of food and nesting materials, which can be dropped out of airplanes for them at convenient locations," said Lila, "as well as big blocks of ice delivered to their homes on a regular basis. I'm going to organize a fundraising drive for that. I could use your help."

"S-s-sure," stammered Stanley. Then he cocked his ear and said, "What's that n-n-noise?"

Lila listened and heard what to her was a familiar sound, unfortunately.

"That's Ranger," she said. "He's always barking his head off. Although this time it sounds like he really means it. I hope he doesn't bust through the fence."

And then, from around the corner, came a boy who Lila and Stanley had never seen before. But they felt they should know him, because he was wearing the school uniform of the Hargrove Academy for the Gifted, Bright, and Perceptive Child, same as they were.

Trailing behind him at a respectful distance was an obedient pack of stray dogs, the kind that usually acted vicious and mean and were always tipping over the trash cans in the neighborhood and making a mess in the street when they weren't terrorizing whoever was unlucky enough to cross their path.

However, with this unknown boy, they all seemed really well behaved, just like the nice dogs that allow you to pet them without biting your hand off.

Ranger was not among them.

The unknown boy noticed Lila and Stanley and stopped, and the dogs that were following him stopped too and grinned and wagged their tails like crazy.

Something about Lila and Stanley had caught the unknown boy's attention. He walked straight up to them.

"Hi," said Lila.

"H-h-hello," stammered Stanley respectfully, who seemed to sense instinctively that this new boy was a Yellow Level student, same as Lila.

"Where'd you guys get those clothes?" demanded Callum.

CHAPTER EIGHT

Callum on the Street

With an earsplitting shriek of its metal brakes, the train had lurched to a stop at an underground den so enormous that it seemed like a whole other world.

"Well, I must say, it was a pleasant change to travel with you and not that awful Billy Bankson," Mrs. T-G remarked to Callum as they prepared to leave the compartment. "I'm fairly sure we'll meet again. My niece goes to school at the Hargrove Academy, and I attend all the school functions. Ah, Charlie, there you are."

The same young man who had helped them on board was carrying two heavy suitcases and trying not to look like it was too much of a strain. Apparently he didn't work for the train company at all, as Callum had initially supposed, but was Mrs. T-G's furless mascot.

"Did I tell you? Charlie works for the Forestry Service," explained Mrs. T-G. "He ran into certain legal problems after he chained himself to a sycamore tree to prevent a bulldozer from destroying the nesting site of a pair of yellow warblers. Now the development company is suing him for every cent he's got. Fortunately, my husband, Luther, the lawyer and former heavyweight boxing champion, has agreed to help him out. Things are looking up for Charlie. As I may have mentioned to you before, Luther has never lost a case."

"Thanks again for that, Mrs. T-G," said Charlie. "And thank your husband again for me, when you get a chance. I'm super grateful."

"Say no more about it," said Mrs. T-G grandly. "I see you have my bags. Thank you. Lead the way. Let's try to beat the rush."

And with that, Charlie and Mrs. T-G slipped out of the train compartment. Callum followed after them and was immediately pushed back by a group of rude and downright inconsiderate people trying to board the train at the same time that he was trying to get off of it.

So many people bumped into him that he thought he was going to lose his mind along with his temper.

I'm *fierce*, he reminded himself for the millionth time lately. I'm *savage*. I am a *wild thing*!

He bared his teeth, made his hands look like deadly claws, and growled like crazy, but no one paid any attention. He was forced to be rude and downright inconsiderate just like everyone else in order to reach the station platform. When he finally got there, he saw no sign of Mrs. T-G or Charlie, only more strangers running to and fro. With no plan at all about what he was going to do, he had no choice but to follow the people who were rushing from the darkened station toward the light of the sunny street above.

The sight that met his eyes when he stepped out onto the street was so incredible that it nearly made his head explode.

Hollow stone mountains reached to the skies, and they must have contained hundreds of dens, judging by the crowds of people going in and coming out of them. Rivers of noisy, smelly machines flowed between the stone mountains, all filled with people too. Some of them were enormous and louder than thunder. And every hundred feet or so, there was a vendor selling more of the rotten, diseased food Mrs. T-G had spoken so disapprovingly about, and so a portion of the various odors floating around were absolutely delicious.

Even though it was still full from breakfast, Callum's stomach sat up and took notice, and his taste buds did too. How he loved everything that was rotten and diseased in this newfangled territory! It was so vastly superior to the rotten and diseased food he was used to in the Wild that it nearly brought a tear to his eye. If only he could have shared some of it with Mom and Dad and Aunt Trudy and Uncle Rick and Grampa, who were accustomed to gorging themselves on tough and stringy meat that they ripped directly off the bone or moldy chunks of carcasses that had been lying around for weeks. One taste of this new and improved kind of rotten and diseased food would probably have put them off of wilderness grub altogether.

Although he wouldn't have minded staying where he was and smelling the delicious rotten food forever, Callum had an instinct to roam, and he traveled along several streets with no rhyme or reason whatsoever. Everywhere he turned, he heard talking. People were talking to each other, they were talking into shiny handheld boxes, and some of them were talking to themselves, with no one else around. They chitchatted. They argued. They were nice to each other, and mean. And the more he listened, the better he was able to understand the words and phrases they used.

I'm getting a pretty good grip on this language thing now, he assured himself proudly, experiencing the same sense of accomplishment that he had felt after grasping the stick to poke out the termites from the decaying log in the woods. More than anything else he had done all day, it made him feel *fierce*.

He also felt sleepy again. All of a sudden, the stress and tension of the day hit him like an Alpha's paw. Even though it was the middle of the day, he had to rest, if only for a moment.

He would have dug a hole in the ground to curl up in, but the ground was covered with an impenetrable sheet of rock. He dragged his weary limbs to a dim, narrow passage behind the nearest tower of metal and stone, crawled into the cleanest, driest sheltered nook he could find, covered himself with pages from an old newspaper that was lying around, and then immediately fell into a deep, dreamless slumber.

City life went on without him, and when he woke up, it was dark out, and his cramped body was as stiff as a board. Things were a lot quieter than before, so much so that the noises that could be heard stood out in an unsettling way. He heard a whispering rustle nearby and some itty-bitty scraping sounds, and his heart jumped into his throat. How silly, to be frightened half to death by something as minor as itty-bitty scraping sounds! Still, he hugged his knees to his chest and curled up into the smallest ball possible. He didn't care enough to look up to see if the moon was out or not. Nighttime was not the same without the pack standing guard.

Thankfully, whatever was making the scraping sounds didn't get any closer, and since he was now too alert to danger to fall asleep again, he passed the time imagining Dad was standing over him, his murderous yellow eyes glittering in a comforting way.

Finally, as it always does, the light of dawn came, and Callum's nighttime fears were banished by the onslaught of morning activity as the city dwellers began their day. The enormous machines came by with their smoke and thunder, and as the noise on the street grew into a regular racket, the mysterious scraping sounds were fortunately lost in the uproar.

He got up, yawned, stretched, scratched his head and various other itches, shook himself all over, and hit the street again, where he quickly traded some of the leftover pocket lettuce from Mrs. T-G with the very first food vendor he met. After bolting down a delicious breakfast of rotten, diseased meat, he felt ten times stronger and three times as brave as before, and continued on his way with a spring in his step.

"Hey, kid!" an angry man in one of the moving machines yelled, after screeching to a stop just a few feet away from him. "I nearly hit ya, ya know! Don't you know a *car* when you see one?"

He was careful to give the machines the right of way after that.

Block by block, he left the colossal inhabited mountains of stone behind and entered a quieter part of the city. Here, the streets were smaller, without so many cars. Leafy green trees grew along the curbs. On every block, big plastic containers with REFUSE/BASURA printed on them were piled high with something that couldn't have been either rotten *or* diseased because it smelled so bad. (Of course, he couldn't read the words, but that's what the shapes of the letters were like.)

On the sidewalk in front of a few of these stinky

REFUSE/BASURA containers he came upon two skinny, dirty dogs viciously fighting over an old, dried-up bone. They were growling and lunging at each other like it was a fight to the death. And the dried-up old bone didn't seem worth it at all.

A worried woman with bright pink curlers in her hair was watching the feud from a window high above the street.

"Help!" she was crying to anyone who would listen, but there was only Callum. "These wild stray dogs run rampant all day and night! It isn't safe for man nor beast! They knock over trash cans and make a mess everywhere! They chase innocent cats! And they're always fighting like crazy over some stupid thing! Someone call the governor! Someone call the president! Someone call the *police*!"

The dogs only fought harder for the dirty old bone. The fur was really starting to fly.

Good grief, Callum thought. This is ridiculous. "Forget about that old bone or learn to share," he told the quarreling rivals sternly. "That's what we did in the pack back where I come from. Haven't you got any manners?"

The dogs only snarled at him savagely. He decided to try to say the same thing the way Dad would have done in the Wild, to the best of his ability. "Bark! Bark!" he growled ferociously. "Yip, yip, yip! Grrr! OwwwooooOOOHHH!"

The stray dogs stopped in midlunge. A look of surprise crossed their faces, then shame. Together they picked up the dried-up old bone and dropped it in front of him. Then they both rolled over onto their backs, exposing their vulnerable throats and undersides.

"Wait," Callum said. "You don't need to do that. I'm not an Alpha Male. I'm just a furless mascot." But since he used his own language to say that, the dogs remained on their backs, waving their filthy paws in the air.

Hmmm, Callum thought. This is weird.

"Well, I'll be," said the woman with the bright pink curlers in her hair, watching it all from her window. "Are those *your* dogs, young man? You should have come by *months* ago. I wouldn't have screamed myself hoarse yelling over and over again for someone to call the police."

Now that the fighting was over, you'd think she'd have turned around and gone back inside to mind her own business, but she lingered at the window waiting to see if anything else would happen that she could scream for help about.

"Here're a few tips," Callum told the stray dogs, using Dad's language again, since it seemed to work so well the first time. "Watch your back. Never spend more time than you need to out in the open. Bones you take straight back to the den. Birds and rabbits you can eat where you find them. If you bring down some big prey, say a caribou or an elk, gorge yourself on raw meat until you think your stomachs are going to explode and then head right back to the den. Got it?"

Of course, in Dad's language it sounded like, "Bark! Bark! Yap, yip, yap! Woof! Woof! Woof! Grrr?"

And with that, Callum continued on his way.

The stray dogs immediately jumped to their feet and followed him, tails wagging like crazy, tongues hanging out of their mouths, ridiculous grins on their faces.

The fight over the dirty old bone, and the bone itself, were completely forgotten.

"You must be *crazy*, barking like that! And your *dogs* are a *nuisance*!" yelled the woman with the bright pink curlers in her hair. "Good riddance to you *all*! And don't come back, or I'm calling the governor, or the president, or the *police*!" Then she finally went back inside and shut the window with a bang.

Now that Callum had met a couple of them, it seemed that everywhere he looked he saw stray dogs on the street. They were all different shapes, all different colors, and all different sizes, but they all had the same joyless look in their narrowed eyes, and the same unhappy, snarling mouths.

Until they heard the ones he had already met bark at them, that is. Then their eyes opened wide, their tails began to wag, and they all started grinning like idiots and following after him.

Soon he was leading a veritable horde of previously terrifying but now pretty tame-looking dogs down the street. People on the sidewalk stopped what they were doing and stared. People in their cars stopped in the middle of the road and stared. Some of the people in the cars honked their horns and waved out their windows.

Callum tried to reason with the growing horde of canines.

"You might find that it helps to break up into smaller packs," he advised them in a series of deep barks, high yips, and low, rumbling growls. "It's easier to get around that way. You really don't want to attract this much attention out in the open. Any prey that wanders by will be warned off long before you can get close enough to do any serious mauling."

But the dogs only wagged their tails harder and grinned at him even more idiotically, and so Callum threw up his hands and continued on his way.

The stray dogs followed after him.

A broad-shouldered man in a dark blue uniform stopped him at the corner.

"Hey, you," he said gruffly. "Do you have a license for those mutts?"

It didn't take a genius to tell that being called "mutts" offended the dogs. They stopped grinning and narrowed their eyes.

"They're not my . . . *dogs*," Callum replied, and they looked at him gratefully, even though he had said it in his own language, not Dad's. And then he tried to walk past the man in the dark blue uniform, but the man put up his hand and stopped him again.

"Whoa, there, sonny," he said. "Not so fast. Don't you know who I am? I'm a police officer, and so you'd better show me some respect and call me sir. Not your dogs, eh? Those mutts sure seem to know you."

"They're only walking down the same street as me, sir," said Callum, making sure the words came out right. Something about the way the police officer was looming over him made him try extra hard. "Same as you are, sir. And they're not your dogs either, I bet."

"*Same as I am?*" repeated the police officer in utter disbelief. "*Not my dogs either?*"

He puffed himself up to appear bigger than he actually was. Obviously he thought he was an Alpha, but Callum could tell he was a Beta at best. True Alphas never needed to puff themselves up to appear bigger than they actually were. They just knew they were bigger than anyone else and left it at that.

Still, Callum was careful not to show any disrespect. Betas were awfully touchy, and they could be dangerous. The slightest thing could set them off, and when they flew off the handle, it was never a pretty sight. Anytime Uncle Rick threw a tantrum, even Aunt Trudy kept out of his way until he cooled down.

The police officer mulled it over, which was something Uncle Rick never did.

"Actually, young man, you are absolutely correct," he said after that. "You are on the street, I am on the street, and those mangy mutts are on the street. Be that as it may, they can't stand around the sidewalk like this, because they're disturbing the peace. They may not be your dogs, and they're certainly not mine, but I want you to walk 'em out of here, pronto. I'll call the pound and have them send the dogcatcher over right away. He'll straighten 'em out but good. Though it might take him two or three trips, there's so many."

"Yes, sir," said Callum and obediently continued on his way down the street.

The gang of stray dogs got up and followed him.

"You see what happens when you hang around too long in the open?" he told them in Dad's harshest barks and growls, to stress the seriousness of the situation. "It only leads to trouble. But you didn't listen to me, did you?"

The stray dogs only grinned and wagged their tails; it looked like a few more of them had shown up and joined the group since the last time he checked. He decided he didn't care whether what he told them sank in or not. All he had to do was keep them together long enough for the dogcatcher from the pound to show up and straighten 'em out but good, like the police officer said.

He had no idea what a dogcatcher was, or what the pound was either, because he had never heard those words before. But he knew these wacky dogs needed to be straightened out. Somewhere along the way, they had missed out on some important information. He had a hard time believing that any of the predators in this ever-growing pack could successfully stalk, attack, and then rip off the head of a moose if its life depended on it. Even Grampa would have turned up his grizzled snout at the dried-up old bone the two dogs were fighting over when Callum first met them, and Grampa would gnaw on just about anything he could find.

Is this what city life is going to do to me? he wondered anxiously. Stunt my growth, and make me so forgetful that I don't even know a good bone when I see one anymore?

"Well, well, looky here!" exclaimed the rude driver of a big gassy car that had stopped in the road across from him. The man had bushy black eyebrows, and he was smoking a fat, smelly cigar.

"How cute!" he said mockingly. "The circus must be in town. It's a doggy parade, and a dopey little redheaded clown is leading the way. Hey, dopey!"

Callum was confused but not exactly offended. Somehow, he knew perfectly well what a circus was, and a clown, and he liked both of those things, but the stray dogs seemed to know what a clown was too, and they didn't like it one bit. They quit grinning and bared their fangs instead.

And then, as if by some mysterious signal, the entire angry horde leaped from the sidewalk and attacked the rude man's car. They clawed at the paint. They chomped on the tires. They jumped on the hood and gnawed on the windshield wipers, all the while making the most terrifying snarling sounds anyone was ever likely to hear in or outside of the Wild.

I guess I judged them too quickly, thought Callum. They could probably bring down a moose with no trouble at all!

"Stop it! I'm sorry. I was only kidding. Hey, give that

back!" cried the rude man. He had dropped his cigar in the street. A savage little stray Chihuahua snatched it up and ran off with it.

"Bring that back!" the man cried again. "I paid a lot of money for that. It's imported!"

The Chihuahua merely dropped the cigar by the curb and then lifted its leg over it.

"Well, now that's going too far," lamented the man.

"Quit it," Callum commanded the rampaging horde. "You should save that kind of assault for when you really need it, like with a caribou or a moose that you can devour afterward."

The stray dogs reacted immediately to the sound of the Wild, and they all ran back to the sidewalk, grinning and wagging their tails, as proud as could be.

The rude man's car looked a fright. It was horribly scratched, and it was clear that the windshield wipers would never do their job again.

"You'll pay for this!" he cried with tears of rage in his eyes. "I'm gonna sue you for every cent you've got. You can't let your dogs attack innocent cars."

"They're not my dogs," replied Callum calmly. "But I'm sorry about your car. They really worked it over, didn't they?"

"I don't believe you!" he retorted. "They *are* your dogs! You called them off in some kind of dog talk, and they obeyed you. Give me your number where you can be reached."

"Try the circus," said Callum, who had a vague notion that he had actually *been* to the circus once or twice and really liked it. "Ask for the dopey redheaded clown."

Even though he didn't say it in Dad's language, the dogs seemed to get a kick out of that.

By this time, the rude man with the bushy black eyebrows had held up traffic for so long that the drivers stuck behind him started honking their horns. "What comes around goes around!" he cried angrily. "You'll get yours one day, you'll see!" He shook his hairy fist in Callum's direction and drove off, and Callum continued on his way, followed closely by his canine crew.

Thinking it over, he decided it was true that what comes around goes around, but in this case the man with the bushy black eyebrows had deserved what had come around to him, since he had brought up the circus and the clown in the first place. And he wasn't too concerned about being sued for every cent he had, since he didn't have any cents, as far as he knew. Still, it was too bad Mrs. T-G wasn't around anymore, because her husband Luther, the lawyer and former heavyweight boxing champion, could really help out if push came to shove. He was helping Charlie from the Forestry Service, after all, and he had never lost a case.

And then Callum turned the corner and saw something that drove every other thought from his mind. Two kids were standing near the stop sign up ahead, and they were wearing navy blue blazers that were identical to the one that Mom had given him.

He couldn't believe his eyes. Had Mom gotten clothes for them too?

CHAPTER NINE

Callum on the Way to School

This is where Callum asked Lila and Stanley where they'd gotten their clothes.

"Where'd you get those dogs?" Lila and Stanley asked in return, both at once.

"I brought them here so that the dogcatcher from the pound can straighten 'em out but good," said Callum.

"N-n-no!" stammered Stanley, sounding horrified.

"That's terrible," said Lila, looking shocked. "How can you be so cruel?"

"Me?" protested Callum. "They're the ones that go around knocking over trash cans and chasing innocent cats."

Wow, he thought proudly. I'm speaking pretty good, er, *well* lately!

"First of all," said Lila, "there *are* no innocent cats. Every cat I've ever known has been guilty of something."

The dogs all grinned and wagged their tails at this and looked like absolute angels.

"Secondly, knocking over trash cans is probably the only way stray dogs know how to get anything to eat," Lila went on sympathetically. "Nobody looks after them at all. The only dogs that ever get released from the city pound are the lucky ones that people adopt, and I'm sorry, but no one in her right mind is going to adopt a troublemaking dog off the street. These strays will be locked up forever, or worse."

Callum could only guess what Lila meant by "worse," and it filled him with dread. He had no idea that the dog-catcher did any such thing with stray dogs. He decided it would be better if he straightened 'em out but good instead. True, they weren't his dogs, but they seemed to mind what he said, when he spoke in Dad's language. It was worth a shot.

"Bark! Bark!" he told them authoritatively. "Yip, yip, ruff, ruff, ruff! Woof, woof, woof! Grrr!"

Or, in other words:

"Listen up! You've got to hightail it out of here like your very lives depend on it, because they do, if my hunch is right about what 'worse' means. Run and hide. Divide into smaller packs. Elect an Alpha Male for each pack, an Alpha Female, a Beta Male, and a Beta Female, and, uh . . ."

He decided to skip the whole Omega thing, considering all of the humiliation that it had caused Grampa.

"Only tip over trash cans in the middle of the night, and

then do it as quietly as you can and clean up the mess afterward," he went on with a few more yips, barks, and growls. "And don't forget to get your whole pack together every once in a while to howl your lungs out at the rising moon, because that's totally fun. Remember that little dogs can help out in a pack just as much as big dogs can, and sometimes even more. Especially savage little stray Chihuahuas. Now scram. Get your packs together, go find some dens, and then stay there until the sun goes down."

Lila and Stanley were astonished to hear Callum growling like a wolf. And they were even more astonished to see the stray dogs take him at his word. Every one of them ran off as fast as its four legs could carry it, yapping excitedly.

"W-w-wow," stammered Stanley, thoroughly impressed. "That must have been some really good advice."

Lila was speechless.

"It wasn't anything anyone else wouldn't have told them, if they knew how to bark," Callum answered modestly.

"Here's our c-c-cab," stammered Stanley.

Lila and Stanley were the only students from the Hargrove Academy that lived on this side of the city, and so a cab came and got them every day. The cabbie popped the trunk, and Lila and Stanley put their rolling tote bags inside. Then Stanley hopped into the backseat, and Lila got in after him. She held the door open for Callum.

"You can ride with us," she said. "There's plenty of room."

"Okay," Callum said and got in the backseat too. He was

glad to be invited. He had never met anyone his own age that was also his own species. It was a nice change of pace.

"Well, well, well! Here we are bright and early on another Tuesday morning," the cabbie said cheerfully. He was wearing a fluffy knit hat, so you couldn't really see his head, and he was wearing big dark sunglasses, so you couldn't really see his eyes. But you could see his mouth as plain as day, and it wore a big, friendly smile.

Callum didn't know what a Tuesday was, but so many things had happened since Mom and Dad and Aunt Trudy and Uncle Rick and Grampa had dropped him off at the edge of the woods that it already seemed like the days in the city were the longest ones he had ever lived through.

"Say," said the cabbie, who could somehow see Callum in the rearview mirror despite his dark glasses, "you're an unfamiliar face. You must be new at the Hargrove Academy, am I right?"

Callum nodded. He felt new everywhere.

"It's an amazing school," said the cabbie supportively. "Full of great achievers. I think you'll like it there. Don't you think so too, Lila?"

"It *is* a g-g-great school," Stanley butted in. Stanley loved the Hargrove Academy almost as much as he loved botany.

"All except for the uniform they make us wear," said Lila. "I hate these dumb blazers."

"I l-l-love my b-b-blazer," stammered Stanley. "It's got the p-p-patch that says 'Hargrove' on it."

"That's some shade of red hair you've got," said the cabbie to Callum. "Just like Lila's. You two could be brother and sister. Am I right?"

Callum looked at Lila. He didn't remember having a sister, but he supposed it was possible. His human family could be anyone and anywhere, for all he knew. They were as much of a mystery to him as the shadowy figures at the back of his mind that he was so mad at. Furious, really.

Lila looked at Callum. Apart from having the same shade of red hair, they didn't look at all alike. His nose was stubby and round like a dog's. Her nose was sharp and pointy. From what she could see, they couldn't possibly be related.

"He m-m-might be Patti P-p-plonsky's brother," said Stanley. "Patti's in the Y-y-yellow Level too, and she's g-g-got red hair, same as L-l-lila's. But P-p-patti and Lila aren't s-s-sisters."

"My goodness, Stanley," said the cabbie. "You've hit on a very important point. People are all brothers and sisters, in a way, even if they're not actually related. We're all members of the human family, am I right? Have you been in town long?" he asked Callum.

"Only yesterday and today," Callum answered.

"Made many new friends yet?"

Callum thought about it. Was Mrs. T-G a friend, or only a benefactor? And was Mr. O'Malley a friend, or just a barber? "Two," he told the cabbie, hoping for the best.

"Two?" the cabbie replied. "Then you'll be happy to know that you're sitting next to two more. And I'll be your friend too, if you let me. My name is Charlie. That makes a total of five friends so far. That's not bad. After all, it's more than the Three Musketeers had, am I right?"

Callum was confused. He already knew a Charlie from the Forestry Service. Was that Charlie his friend too? "Thank you," he said politely, wondering how many Charlies he would be expected to meet in the city.

"We haven't been introduced yet," said Lila, sounding a little embarrassed to be doing it so late. "I'm Lila."

"I'm S-s-stanley," said Stanley.

"My name is Clam," said Callum, "like the mollusk."

He still hadn't remembered that his real name was Callum.

"C-c-cool," said Stanley. "You'll have to m-m-meet Salmon. She's in the Green Level. And T-t-tadpole. He's in the B-b-blue Level. They're both really nice."

"Parents today," sighed Charlie the cabbie.

"I can guess who one of your friends is," said Lila to Callum. "It's Billy Bankson, isn't it? He's in the Yellow Level, same as me. You're wearing a button just like the one he's always got on. You must belong to the same club or something."

"It's the peace symbol," explained Callum. "It's for believers in worldwide disarmament."

"Maybe you should remind Billy about that sometime,"

said Lila. "He only wears it because it makes him look good."

Callum wondered if it made him look good too.

"What Lila m-m-means is that it makes Billy seem like a b-b-better person than he actually is," Stanley clarified. "Someone who actually c-c-cares about other people besides himself."

"Which Billy never does," said Lila.

Clearly Lila and Stanley didn't like Billy Bankson very much. Neither did Mrs. T-G. Callum got the mental picture of a rabid skunk in a navy blue blazer with a peace symbol button on it, lifting its obnoxious tail in every direction.

"I don't see why all you guys can't be better friends," said Charlie. "All you need is a little PLU—Peace, Love, and Understanding. Am I right?"

None of the kids in the backseat made any reply, Callum because he had nothing to say, Lila and Stanley because they were being polite. They'd heard about peace, love, and understanding from Charlie before. He'd never met Billy Bankson. Billy had a driver of his own. He didn't take any cabs.

"You're in the Yellow Level, aren't you?" Lila told Callum in a way that made it seem that he was. Callum didn't know anything about the Yellow Level, but he supposed she ought to know what she was talking about. There was something very Alpha about her.

"How did you know that?" he asked.

"I c-c-called it!" stammered Stanley, who could always spot a Yellow Level student.

"Because you're friends with Billy Bankson," Lila replied matter-of-factly. "He's in the Yellow Level. So am I."

"I'm only in the B-B-Blue Level," stammered Stanley.

"That may be, but you're tall enough to be in the Purple Level already, Stanley," said Charlie, which made Stanley feel good, although it made him a little nervous too. After all, he was still growing. How tall would he get? Taller than a building? Was that possible?

Of course, Callum had never met Billy Bankson, but he wasn't about to disagree with Lila. She had Alpha certainty.

"How's your report on the polar bears and the penguins coming along, Lila?" asked Charlie. "You may not know this, Clam, my friend," he went on, "but the word on the street is that the polar ice caps are melting and the polar bears and the penguins need our help to survive. Lila's been pretty broken up about it."

Callum didn't know what polar ice caps were, or what polar bears and penguins were either, but he had some experience with grizzly bears, and if polar bears were anything like grizzly bears, he would say it was better not to have anything to do with them at all, no matter how much help they needed. Bears had too much attitude. One of them could be talking with you as friendly as could be, and then all of a sudden it would want to knock your head off with a swipe of its mighty paw.

On more than one occasion, Dad and Mom and Aunt Trudy and Uncle Rick took all the time and trouble to bring down an elk or a caribou, and just when dinner was ready Grampa would put back his ears and mutter, "Oh, great. Look who showed up," and Dad would lash his tail angrily and say, "Darn it all anyway," and Callum would look up to see a big old grizzly bear sitting down to eat.

"I hope you don't mind if I join you," he would say in a deep bass growl that caused Callum's chest to rattle.

"Of course not, Roger," Mom would reply with a whimper. "Make yourself at home."

Dad would snarl under his breath, Aunt Trudy and Uncle Rick would force a smile, and Grampa would simply lie down and put his paws over his snout and moan.

"In that case, I'm sure you won't mind if I include Estelle and the kids," the grizzly would say.

"How did I know that was coming?" Dad would growl, rolling his eyes.

"Estelle, honey, come on out here. And bring Roger Junior and little Caprice," the grizzly bear would call out, and crashing out from the brush would come an enormous female grizzly and two huge grizzly cubs.

At which point, Dad and Mom and Aunt Trudy and Uncle Rick and Grampa and Callum would get up and head back to the den, and the grizzly bear family wouldn't even notice they were gone.

So Callum wasn't too sympathetic where bears were

concerned. Maybe polar bears were more considerate than grizzlies, but he doubted it. As for penguins, he had never met one, so he wished them well.

"I'm organizing a fundraising drive," said Lila, "to help pay for care packages of food and nesting materials that can be dropped out of airplanes for them at convenient locations, among other things."

"C-c-count me in," stammered Stanley.

"Me too," piped up Charlie.

"It's just a proposal," Lila said modestly. "That's all our assignment calls for." She turned to Callum. "I know you're new and all, but you'll probably still have to do it. It's for life sciences. Mr. Sears is pretty strict."

"Do what?" Callum asked.

"Write a five-hundred-word report on the plight of two of the world's endangered species and propose a program to provide some relief for them," said Lila.

"That's so c-c-cool," stammered Stanley yet again. It was about the only thing he ever said when it came to the Yellow Level.

At first, Callum hadn't understood what Lila meant, but then he thought about it and decided that he knew what endangered meant and what relief was. The most endangered species he'd come across lately were the stray dogs that were running for their lives from the dogcatcher. They could certainly use some relief.

He was wondering what a five-hundred-word report was

when Charlie stopped the cab and said, "Here we are, guys. The Hargrove Academy for the Gifted, Bright, and Perceptive Child. The three of you qualify on all counts, I'm happy to say. I'll meet you back here in the lineup at three o'clock sharp. Have fun!"

CHAPTER TEN

Callum at School

A businessman by the name of Phineas G. Hargrove founded the Hargrove Academy for the Gifted, Bright, and Perceptive Child in 1942.

Phineas G. Hargrove had been roommates in college with a young man named Morris B. Peabody. Morris B. Peabody was in the habit of leaving notes and reminders to himself on the refrigerator door using little magnets glued to colorful bits of plastic and painted wood, which he made by himself in his spare time. Phineas G. Hargrove stole this idea from him and convinced his father Tiberius J. Hargrove, who manufactured doorknobs, to manufacture refrigerator magnets of all shapes, sizes, and colors instead. In seven years Phineas G. Hargrove was a millionaire, and Morris B. Peabody was selling cleaning supplies door to door and barely scraping out a living.

Phineas G. Hargrove didn't give two hoots about that,

and he never gave Morris B. Peabody a single nickel for his idea.

The only thing Phineas G. Hargrove cared about more than stealing other people's ideas and making money from them was having people think he was a great and noble man, so when he was supervising the construction of his Academy for the Gifted, Bright, and Perceptive Child, he made certain to reserve a spot right in front of the building where he could place a statue of himself looking very great and noble indeed.

He put a big sign on the statue's pedestal that said:

PHINEAS G. HARGROVE,
INVENTOR OF THE REFRIGERATOR MAGNET

In recent years the pedestal had been repeatedly vandalized. With the addition of some silver spray paint, the sign now read:

PHINEAS G. HARGROVE,
INVENTOR OF THE REFRIGERATOR MAGNET—*NOT*

Mr. Rutgers, the janitor, scoured the pedestal clean every day, but the added word was always there the next morning. And this was the first thing that Callum saw when Charlie dropped him and Lila and Stanley off at school that morning.

"That's old man Hargrove, looking great and noble,"

said Lila. "But he didn't really invent the refrigerator magnet. That's what the 'not' is for. He stole the idea from his roommate in college."

Callum nodded wisely, although he hadn't a clue what she was talking about. Everyone else at school knew the story about poor Morris B. Peabody ever since a Hargrove graduate had published his biography, titled *Morris B. Peabody, the True Inventor of the Refrigerator Magnet*. It was important to this Hargrove graduate to set the record straight. His name was Milton K. Peabody, and he was the grandson of Morris B. Peabody's brother Franklin O. Peabody.

Unfortunately, it didn't do Morris B. Peabody any good, since he had disappeared without a trace long ago, after giving up on everything and moving to Mexico.

In the meantime, however, the Hargrove Academy for the Gifted, Bright, and Perceptive Child became famous for the amazing accomplishments of its gifted, bright, and perceptive students, many of whom went on to lead the world in the arts and sciences. Every now and then, one of its student projects was so advanced that it was classified top secret by the federal government. Those projects earned an automatic A.

"How much do you already know about the way things work around here?" Lila asked Callum. "Has anyone told you anything about it yet?"

"Nobody's told me anything," replied Callum.

"Well," said Lila, "first of all, we've got homeroom with

Mr. Rutledge, and that's when we catch up with homework. And then he teaches language arts and writing perspectives. And then Mr. Hervey teaches math and computer skills. And then Ms. Capin teaches geography and social studies, and then Mr. Sears teaches either earth sciences or life sciences. On Mondays, Wednesdays, and Fridays, we go to PE with Ms. King. On Tuesdays and Thursdays, and then every other Friday . . . oh, here we are."

Lila led Callum into a classroom in which neat wooden desks stood in five orderly rows. Each desk seemed to belong to someone already.

"Those two in the back corner are free," Lila advised Callum. "Mr. Rutledge should be here any minute." A tall, flustered man entered the room. "Wait," Lila said. "That's not Mr. Rutledge. It's a substitute. You'd better hold on to your hat. Things are going to get a little crazy around here."

"All right, everybody, settle down. Take your seats, please," said the tall, flustered man, and Callum sat down at an empty corner desk in the back row.

"Excuse me, sir," said a boy sitting a couple of desks away from Callum. "May I go to the restroom, please?"

A couple of other boys smirked at this, but Callum didn't see why.

"Not now. The bell just rang," replied the tall, flustered man, sitting at Mr. Rutledge's desk. A big, painted picture tacked on the wall behind it proclaimed WE LOVE MR. RUT-LEDGE! The substitute anxiously shuffled through a bunch of papers that were strewn on the desk.

"Settle down, please," he told the class again. "My name is Mr. Abrams. I'm your guest teacher for today, and I'm very happy to be here."

"What's wrong with Mr. Rutledge?" asked a bright-eyed girl in the front row, clutching her hands together in heartfelt concern.

"I don't know that anything is wrong with Mr. Rutledge," said Mr. Abrams. "I just know that he won't be in today for some reason."

"He wasn't feeling very well yesterday," said the girl in the front row.

"Well, then, I suppose he's feeling worse today, poor guy," said Mr. Abrams. "We'll all have to hope he gets better and pray that we don't catch the same thing that laid him low. We'll take roll in a second, just as soon as I can find the class list."

And he went back to searching through the papers on Mr. Rutledge's desk.

The three boys who Callum saw smirking immediately got up and forced three girls to trade desks with them, so that they could sit near the boy who had asked to visit the restroom. All four of the boys then smirked some more.

"Ha-ha, I found it!" said Mr. Abrams triumphantly, waving a sheet of paper in the air.

"Please, sir," said the boy who had asked to visit the restroom. He had stopped smirking and wore an earnest expression on his face. "I really have to go."

"Don't believe him, sir," said one of the three girls who

had been forced to leave their seats. "He's lying. He always takes advantage of the substitutes." Clearly it took an effort for her to rat anyone out. Her voice sounded shaky and nervous. But she was mad enough at being forced to leave her desk that she couldn't help but speak up.

"I am *not* lying," said the boy who wanted to visit the restroom.

"*You are too*," said the girl who had been forced to trade seats.

"Please, no more 'sir.' Call me Mr. Abrams," said Mr. Abrams, who was still a young man and hadn't really gotten used to being called "mister" yet, let alone "sir." "And no one is allowed to leave this room until I have taken roll," he added. "Becca Adams."

"Here," said the bright-eyed girl in the front row.

"Jose Alvarez," said Mr. Abrams.

"Here," said the boy who wanted to visit the restroom.

"Excuse me, sir," said Becca. "I mean, Mr. Abrams. He's not Jose Alvarez. He's Billy Bankson. That's Jose over there," she said, pointing to one of the boys who had taken another girl's desk, "sitting at Rachel Cohen's desk."

"It's not Rachel's desk," said the boy she'd pointed out.

"*It is too*," said Rachel Cohen. "And I want it *back*."

"I'm not Jose Alvarez," protested the boy. "I'm Billy Bankson."

The boy who wanted to visit the restroom laughed. He and the boy who claimed to be Billy Bankson raised their hands and high-fived each other.

Callum was getting dizzy. Obviously, keeping track of who was who in this class was going to be a major chore.

"As long as both Jose and Billy are here, I don't especially care who is who," said Mr. Abrams, who looked like he was getting pretty dizzy too. "But I was planning on allowing Billy Bankson to visit the restroom when I'm through taking roll, not Jose Alvarez."

"Score!" said the boy who supposedly stole Rachel's desk.

"Ha, ha, you got me," said the boy who had asked to visit the restroom. "I'm Billy Bankson after all. Not him. He *is* Jose Alvarez."

"I told you, sir," said Becca Adams to Mr. Abrams. "I mean, Mr. Abrams."

"Can I go to the restroom now, please?" asked Billy.

"You may go when I'm through taking roll," said Mr. Abrams, and then continued down the class list. Billy Bankson and his friends made a rude comment under their breath about each and every name he called, and then they smirked like crazy.

"Quiet, please," said Mr. Abrams. "I don't want to take names, but I will if I have to."

Billy and his friends were as quiet as they could be for a few minutes after that.

"Please, sir, may I go to the restroom now?" asked Billy after Mr. Abrams had called Amy Zell. Amy was absent, as usual. Her mother acted in movies, and she was always taking Amy out of school for photo opportunities.

"Amy is in Puerto Vallarta, Mr. Abrams," said Becca.

"I wish I were," said Mr. Abrams frankly.

"Please, sir," said Billy again. "You said I could go after roll was called."

"Yes, I did," said Mr. Abrams. "I'm a man of my word." He wrote Billy a pass. "Drop this class list off at the front office for me while you're at it, would you, please?"

"Sure," said Billy, grinning wildly.

One of Billy's friends had kicked Lila out of her desk too. There was nothing she could do about it. It never paid to fight back against Billy Bankson and his gang of reprobates. They only bothered you more if you did. She was sitting now at a desk near the back row.

"Mr. Abrams didn't call your name," she told Callum quietly. "Shouldn't you say something? You don't want to be marked absent when you're actually here."

"I guess so," said Callum, but he didn't raise his hand.

"Excuse me, Mr. Abrams," said Lila, speaking up for him. "You didn't call Clam's name. Clam, like the mollusk."

"My goodness," said Mr. Abrams. "That's an unusual name."

"Not at this school," said Becca.

"I see," said Mr. Abrams. "And who in this class is named Clam, like the mollusk?"

"I am," said Callum.

"Well, you're here all right," said Mr. Abrams. "I can see that plain enough. Are you new?"

"Yes," replied Callum.

"Well, I must have picked up an old class list by mistake," said Mr. Abrams. "I suppose I'm lucky I found one at all. I'll mark you down and hope for the best. What's your surname?"

Surname? Callum drew a blank.

"That means last name," Becca informed Callum. Then she said to Mr. Abrams, "It's okay that he doesn't know what surname means. He wasn't here for Names Day, when we learned all about it."

"Thank you, Becca," said Mr. Abrams and looked at Callum expectantly.

Still Callum said nothing. Nothing came to mind.

"You must have some other name than Clam, like the mollusk," Mr. Abrams said, trying to draw him out. "Can't you tell me what it is?"

Again Callum had no answer. Mr. Abrams looked at him like he was a jack-in-the-box that could pop out at any moment. The Hargrove Academy was famous for attracting the most gifted, the brightest, and the most perceptive students for miles around. Brilliant people had their quirks.

Callum thought about it. Mom used to call him "Pig Face" and "Salty Lollipop," but he didn't really think that either one of those names was his surname. The closest thing to a proper name that anyone in the family ever had for him was Firehead. Aunt Trudy even called him Firehead when she was complaining about what a burden he was to the family, although she dedicated most of her energies to ignoring him completely.

"Firehead," he told Mr. Abrams after a moment or two. "My name is Clam Firehead."

"Firehead?" repeated Mr. Abrams as if he couldn't believe it. Then he said, "Clam Firehead. That makes two unusual names."

"Firehead sounds Native American," Becca remarked smartly. "We have two Native American students here at school. One is in the Orange Level, and one is in the Green Level."

"The Hargrove Academy is fortunate indeed to have so many gifted, bright, and perceptive students and such diversity," said Mr. Abrams, looking and sounding more than a little dizzy now. "It's a credit to the institution of education."

At which point, Billy Bankson returned to class. "Look what I got from the vending machine," he bragged to Jose. "Sunflower seeds. And you can't have any." He took his seat and began making farting noises with his hand against his armpit, to the delight of his friends.

Callum didn't know what sunflower seeds were, but he understood the farting noises well enough. Grampa would fit right in around here, he decided.

"Quiet, please," said Mr. Abrams. "Let's proceed to our language arts lesson. Since Mr. Rutledge left me no instructions that I can find, we're going to analyze a little poem that I'm going to have to come up with off the top of my head."

He picked up a pen and wrote on the dry-erase board, THE POLICE HAVE BEEN CALLED / AND THEY'LL SET UP A DRAGNET / TO FIND OUT WHO STOLE / THE REFRIGERATOR MAGNET, and then he read it aloud.

"I didn't steal any refrigerator magnets!" Billy declared loudly, and then he and his friends laughed uproariously.

"Settle down," said Mr. Abrams. "I'm not accusing anyone. I'm simply putting this up on the board for the purpose of discussion. Now, what do you think is the first and most obvious thing that you can say about this poem in terms of its construction?"

"It's a lie," interrupted Billy Bankson again. "Because I'm innocent!"

Once more he and his friends laughed uproariously.

"Settle down," said Mr. Abrams stoically. "Eyes on the board, if you please."

Honestly, thought Callum, what did Mr. Abrams expect? If he wanted to be treated like an Alpha Male, he ought to act like one. Instead of drooping like a wet leaf of grass, he should stand stiff-legged and tall. His ears should be erect and forward, and his hackles should bristle. That's the way Dad always did it, and nobody ever talked back to Dad.

"Excuse me, Mr. Abrams, Billy keeps interrupting, and it's preventing me from fully concentrating on the lesson," said Becca, stating the obvious.

"Thank you, Becca," said Mr. Abrams wearily. "I think Billy is aware that his actions are distracting the class. I'm afraid that I'm going to have to write down his name for Mr. Rutledge."

"No, no, no!" cried Billy. "I'm not doing anything wrong. I'm being good."

"Well, let's keep it that way," said Mr. Abrams. "Now, let me ask you again. What is the most obvious thing about this poem in terms of its construction, do you think? Yes," he said, pointing to a shy, pudgy boy wearing glasses that looked too big for his head. "What's your name again?"

"Tito Jones," said the boy.

"All right, Tito, can you tell me what you think is the most obvious thing about this poem in terms of its construction?" asked Mr. Abrams.

"It's about someone who stole a refrigerator magnet," replied Tito.

A few rows behind him, Billy could barely contain himself.

"*Ha ha ha!*" he guffawed, giving in to his worst impulse.

"Billy, what did I tell you?" said Mr. Abrams.

"Sorry," said Billy. "I'll be good. I promise."

"What you said is certainly true, Tito," said Mr. Abrams, "but that has to do with the *subject matter* of the poem, not its *construction*."

He wrote the words SUBJECT MATTER and CONSTRUCTION on opposite sides of the dry-erase board.

"The subject matter is what the poem is about," explained Mr. Abrams. "The construction is how the poem is put together. Thank you, Tito, for helping us make that distinction."

"You're welcome," said Tito.

"So can anyone tell me what they think the most obvious thing about this poem is in terms of its construction?" asked Mr. Abrams. "Yes," he said, pointing to Lila, who had her hand up.

"It rhymes," answered Lila. "'Dragnet' rhymes with 'magnet.'"

"Very good," said Mr. Abrams. "The most obvious thing about any poem in terms of its construction is whether it rhymes or not. Some poems do, and some don't. This one does."

Callum looked at Lila admiringly. She was definitely as smart as she looked.

"Poems are stupid!" Billy snickered, who could no longer contain his bad self.

"That one is really stupid!" giggled Jose.

They and their friends all started laughing their heads off.

"All right, boys," said Mr. Abrams. "You've pushed me too far. I'm writing down your names for Mr. Rutledge."

This time it had no effect whatsoever. Billy and his friends continued to cut up and cause trouble all the way until lunch.

Mr. Abrams collapsed into his chair at the sound of the bell.

"*Thank the Lord,*" he said loudly.

Callum had spent most of the morning feeling completely dumbfounded, but by lunchtime there was one thing he had learned at school so far. Some poems rhymed, and others didn't, and that was the first thing you could tell about them.

CHAPTER ELEVEN
Callum at Lunch

When it rained in the Wild, the air smelled like wet wood. In the city, Callum noticed, it smelled like wet cement.

He liked both of those smells.

"We get forty minutes for lunch. This is the school cafeteria," explained Lila and led him around the puddles in the courtyard to a white-painted hall filled with rows of long wooden tables.

"This week, the Red Level, the Orange Level, the Yellow Level, and the Silver Level have first lunch," she said. "Next week, we switch with the Gold Level, the Green Level, the Blue Level, and the Purple Level. Since you didn't bring anything, I suppose you're planning on buying your food. I'll show you where to go."

Callum knew about buying food. He pulled out the leftover pocket lettuce Mrs. T-G had given him and showed it to Lila.

"That's enough money for sure," she said. "It's not very expensive here. Most of the food we get is donated by the Association of Organic Farmers of America. Today is Tuesday, so you've got the choice of veggie hot dogs or sloppy joes. I brought some carrot sticks and soy cheese spread, but I want to get an apple juice and a side of mashed potatoes, so I'll go up to the counter with you."

They each took a tray and joined the line. Again he smelled the intoxicating aroma of food that was rotten and diseased, in the words of Mrs. T-G.

Lila seemed to know exactly what Mrs. T-G had meant about that.

"Yuck!" she said disgustedly. "Those meaty sloppy joes smell so rotten and diseased that I can hardly stand it!"

Callum's stomach did a backflip. He made his choice right there. "Sloppy joes," he told the woman behind the counter enthusiastically, and she served him a heaping plate.

"Another carnivore," Lila said with a sigh, sounding disappointed but used to it.

Callum wondered how she would react to the sight of Mom and Dad and Aunt Trudy and Uncle Rick and Grampa burying their snouts in a disemboweled elk, ravenously devouring all sorts of bloody raw organs and body parts.

"There are tables outside," said Lila, "but since it's raining, we'd better eat in here."

She led the way to where her friends sat. Callum recognized them all from class that morning. There was the bright-eyed girl from the front row, the shy, pudgy boy with the glasses that looked too big for his face, a girl with glossy hair and shiny silver braces on her teeth, and a skinny boy with almond eyes.

"Becca Adams, Tito Jones, Rachel Cohen, Curtis Takahashi, this is Clam Firehead," Lila said, introducing him to the group. "In case you don't know it, it's his first day here."

"Hi, Clam," they all said.

"I like your metal teeth," he told Rachel right away, admiring her shiny braces.

No one had ever complimented Rachel on her braces before, although plenty of people had made fun of them or ignored them politely.

"Thanks," she replied, a little confused. "I think. I like your name."

"It's Native American, isn't it?" asked Becca as if she already knew the answer was yes.

"You could really tear into a tough animal hide with chompers like those," said Callum to Rachel. He still wasn't over being impressed.

Luckily, Rachel was an omnivore or she might have taken offense. Omnivores eat everything. "I suppose so," she said shyly, being the good sport that she was. "Although I'm super careful about biting into anything tough. I don't like to get anything caught in the brackets."

Callum was not surprised to hear this. Despite her fierce teeth, Rachel was clearly one of several Omega members in this pack. Strangely, he couldn't spot a Beta anywhere. This was the first pack he had ever heard of to have two Alpha Females, namely Becca and Lila, and all the rest Omegas.

Callum had only ever been a furless mascot. If he expected to fill the Alpha Male position one day, he would need training. He thought about how to make the best of the situation. Perhaps he could start in Omega position and then move up to Beta, but it was plain to see that there were too many Omegas in Lila's pack already. He couldn't try out for Beta Male when there was no Alpha Male. The only status position available in Lila's pack was Beta Female. And that was obviously out of the question.

Meanwhile, his lunch was getting cold. He lowered his head and said grace.

"Oh Great Spirit that guides the Sun and Moon and Lights the Stars and watches over All That Lives in This World and Beyond," he said reverently, "I thank You for this nourishing meal, and the Association of Organic Farmers of America also."

This surprised everyone at the table, and not just because he had said it without making a single mistake.

"That was simply beautiful," said Rachel with a smile that made her silver braces shine like the sun.

"He's so spiritual," said Becca approvingly.

Callum didn't hear them. He was oblivious to everything else as he buried his snout in his deliciously rotten and diseased sloppy joe.

"Man, you really like that stuff, don't you?" said Curtis Takahashi, sounding impressed in a different way. "You can have the rest of mine, if you want it. The food they serve here makes me gag. I'd rather forage for nuts and berries."

"Here's mine," said Tito Jones, pushing his tray forward. "I'd rather forage for nuts and berries too."

There was a terrible commotion at the opposite end of the room.

"Who is it this time?" asked Becca, sounding bored.

"Take a guess," said Lila.

Across the room, a boy that Callum had never seen was shaking in rage. "Give it back!" he shouted. He was small and skinny and a hunk of hair so blond it was almost white stuck out from the top of his head. His eyes were wet with tears and his face was as red as a cherry.

Omega again, Callum thought automatically.

"Give it back!" the boy cried a second time. "That's *my* pudding!"

"Not anymore!" cried Billy Bankson in return, standing two feet away from him. "It's mine now!"

He tossed the sealed plastic pudding container to Jose Alvarez, who caught it single-handedly like the excellent ballplayer he was.

"That's not fair!" cried the red-faced boy. "Sloppy joes make me sick, and veggie hot dogs smell like dirty socks! If I don't have my pudding, I won't have any lunch at all!"

"So go on a diet already," said Billy. "You're big enough

as it is, fatty. You could stand to lose a few pounds." And the boys at his table all hooted and laughed.

"What a jerk," said Becca.

"Yeah, he's a real caveman," said Tito. "I'm glad I'm not sitting over there." He shuddered.

"It's not entirely his fault," Lila said understandingly, looking at Billy like he was a pathetic baby bird that had fallen out of its nest. "His mom and dad are always going to the South of France, and they leave him behind without any supervision. The only people he's got at home are the housekeeper and his driver, and they let him do whatever he wants whenever he wants to instead of enforcing the boundaries that he so desperately needs. That's why he runs around like a maniac and never thinks about anyone except himself. He's growing up all helter-skelter, like a weed."

"My heart bleeds for him," said Becca sarcastically.

"I think he should be locked up," said Rachel. "And they should throw away the key."

Callum didn't hear a single word they said. If there was one thing he could spot from a mile away, it was an Alpha Male. He immediately picked up his tray and headed off to the opposite end of the room.

I'm *fierce*, he reminded himself. I'm *savage*. I am a *wild thing*!

"What on earth is he doing?" he heard Becca say behind him.

"I haven't a clue," said Lila.

"He didn't take my sloppy joe," said Tito. "Does anyone else want it?"

Callum walked straight over to the table where Billy and his friends sat. Along the way, he snarled at five easy-to-spot Omegas and snatched their puddings away from them. True to form, they merely rolled over and accepted their fate.

"What do you know?" he heard Becca say loudly. "Clam's a jerk too!" Not knowing what a jerk was, he took it as a compliment and vowed to be the best jerk the school had ever seen.

"I don't understand," he heard Lila say. She sounded confused. "There must be some explanation."

He felt it was a strange reaction for an Alpha to have. What's so hard to understand about the survival of the fittest? It's the rule of the Wild!

He had learned enough from Uncle Rick not to pussyfoot around in situations like this, so he boldly elbowed his way into taking a seat directly across from the Alpha at Billy's table.

"What the hey?" complained Jose, who had received the business end of his elbow.

"Here you go," said Callum, depositing the pudding containers in front of Billy.

"Holy moly," said Billy, impressed. "Good job, man!"

"Who do you think you are?" demanded Jose.

Callum recognized a Beta Male challenge when he saw one.

"I'm Clam," he said. "Like the mollusk. And I foraged for puddings way better than you ever could."

"Foraged?" asked Jose warily. "What's that?"

As well as being a top ballplayer, Jose was a genius at math. He had already mastered trigonometry and calculus and was working on some equations that nobody had ever thought of before. But his vocabulary needed working on, as did his social skills.

"I've got a heap of pudding now, that's for sure," said Billy greedily. "More than anyone ever dreamed of. And I don't even like the stuff!"

Whether Billy liked pudding or not made no difference to Callum. He had foraged for the whole pack. Along with Jose, there was a big hulking boy with a single eyebrow stretched across his forehead where most people had two, and a good-looking black guy who Callum suspected could successfully challenge Billy for the Alpha Male position anytime he wanted to.

"That's Jose Alvarez, that's John Mason, and that's Roger Phipps," said Billy. "And I'm Billy Bankson."

"I know who you are," said Callum, and went back to gobbling up his sloppy joe.

"Holy moly," said Billy again, in amazement. "You really like that stuff?"

"'Course I do," said Callum. "It's rotten and diseased, isn't it?"

The whole pack laughed loudly at this.

"You got that right," said Roger Phipps. "You can have mine too, if you want it."

Callum held out his hand and took Roger's plate.

"Holy moly," said Billy once more. "You are hard-core, dude. Here, take mine!"

Everyone watched Callum devour a whole mess of sloppy joes as if they couldn't believe it.

As much as he knew about packs and their ways, Callum had to admit that he was a little perplexed. Either city predators had it really, really easy, or they just didn't realize how hard it was to survive to maturity and beyond. Mom and Dad and Aunt Trudy and Uncle Rick and Grampa would never dream of abandoning a carcass until they had stripped it clean of every ounce of sustenance. They never knew when the next prey was going to fall victim to their razor-sharp teeth and deadly claws.

Billy noticed the button pinned to Callum's navy blue blazer, the one with the picture of what looked like a little tree growing upside-down.

"That's a cool button," he said. "It's the peace symbol, right? I used to have one just like it, but I lost it when some wiseacre stole my rucksack up in the woods."

He looked at Jose accusingly. "*Some wiseacre*," he said again, meaningfully.

"How many times do I have to tell you? It wasn't me!" Jose said defensively.

"Hargrove has a lodge by the National Forest," Roger

Phipps explained to Callum. "Once a month or so, one of the Levels gets to go up for the weekend and commune with Nature. There are some dorms with bunks and stuff, and an amphitheater. It's pretty cool, if you're into that kind of thing. We were just there this weekend."

"If only every nation on earth followed the peace symbol," Billy said fervently, as if he could make it happen simply by wishing for it hard enough, "there would be no more war, no more oppression, and no more persecution. People would learn to live together as friends, not enemies. And everyone would love one another."

He stood up.

"All right, widgets," he instructed forcefully, addressing the Omegas in the lunchroom. "Listen up. Anyone who wants their pudding back can buy it from me for fifty cents. Anyone who doesn't buy their pudding back can expect to meet me in the corridor after lunch and pay the consequences instead. Anyone who doesn't have enough money to buy their pudding back had better get it and fast."

He sat down again.

"Yeah," he said as if nothing had happened. "World peace would be so great."

"You said it, Billy. There's nothing like matching your actions to your words," said Roger, rolling his eyes toward the ceiling.

In less than a minute there were three dollars and fifty

cents in quarters on the table, because Billy forced one of the helpless Omegas to buy Billy's pudding as well as his own. Counting the five that Callum had foraged and the one that Billy had already stolen from the little blond boy, that added up to a total of seven.

Callum had wondered where pocket lettuce came from, and the metal coins it bred, and now it seemed he had the answer. It came from other people!

"Tell you what, I'll give you a dollar," Billy said to Callum. "After all, you earned it. You did almost as much work as I did getting all that pudding together."

"Yeah, almost," said Roger, being sarcastic again.

"You never shared any money with *me*," complained Jose. "Or anything else either."

"Or *me*," said John Mason.

Roger Phipps was the only one who didn't appear to give a hoot about the pudding or the money.

"Quit your whining," said Billy. "You sound like a couple of old alley cats when somebody steps on their tails."

Jose and John stared down at their plates looking miserable. Lunch was nearly over now. Students who had finished eating were busing their trays. Billy spent his time trying to trip the people who were walking by.

"Ha-ha!" he laughed delightedly again and again. "Got you!"

Suddenly Lila appeared at the table. "I see you've reunited with your friends, Clam Firehead," she said coldly.

"I hope you'll be happy hanging out with the meanest and most inconsiderate guys in the Yellow Level."

Billy, Jose, and John all laughed in her face. Roger looked away as if he were embarrassed.

Lila stood her ground. Callum had to admire her. She was an Alpha, no doubt about it. But he was confused again, for the millionth time that day. Had he hurt her feelings somehow? He hadn't meant to do that.

"You're a disgrace," said Becca Adams, who had appeared at Lila's side to lend moral support. "And after you said that beautiful prayer about the Great Spirit. I just can't believe it!"

Both girls then turned on their heels and marched out of the lunchroom.

"Man, you *are* good," said Billy to Callum admiringly. "Those girls are too much. They think they're so special. You really know how to push their buttons!"

Jose, John, and Roger got up and cleared their trays. Billy took Callum aside.

"Listen," he said conspiratorially. "I feel like cutting class for the rest of the day. How about you? I'm gonna call James, my driver, and make him pick me up. Why don't you come along? We'll have some laughs."

"Okay," said Callum.

You did it, he told himself matter-of-factly. Beta status was within his grasp.

CHAPTER TWELVE
Callum Plays Hooky

Over here," said Billy. "What are you doing? Get down, like this!"

He stooped low and scurried along the hedgerow at the back of the school like a beetle.

Callum stooped low and followed him.

"That's so we don't get spotted if anyone looks out the window," said Billy.

"So what if they catch us?" Callum asked innocently.

"Man, you are *so* hard-core," said Billy, which was the highest compliment he could think of. "You don't care at all about getting in trouble, do you? You should cut class with me more often."

It had never occurred to Callum that what they were doing could get them in trouble. Until now, he'd thought students were allowed to leave school whenever they wanted to. Cutting class didn't worry him, though. Billy could do no wrong, as far as he was concerned. Alpha Males made their own rules sometimes. It came with the territory.

A long, sleek black car was waiting in the alleyway.

"That's our ride," said Billy. He got in the back of the car and motioned for Callum to follow. "We're safe now," he said when they were both inside and he had slammed the door shut. "Try to get us now, suckers!" he yelled out the window. Then he said to Callum, "Let's hit the park, okay?"

"Okay," said Callum. It had stopped raining. The sun was peeking through the clouds. The air smelled fresh and clean. He thought it would be nice to go anywhere, as long as it was outdoors.

"To the park, James," Billy said sharply to the man in the driver's seat, who was busy doing something with his hands.

"James is always text messaging somebody on his cell phone. He can't live without it," Billy explained to Callum, then turned to the driver again and spoke more loudly. "I said, to the park, James. Sometime today would be great."

"Huh? Oh, right. You got it, buddy. Let me just text good-bye to my friend," James said amiably, and the long, sleek black car moved down the alley.

A few minutes later, the car pulled up to the park.

"Have fun, guys," said James to Billy and Callum. Then he yelled out the window, "Keep your shirt on, buddy!" This was because the person in the car behind them was honking the horn at him.

"Call me when you need picking up," he said to Billy. He

didn't seem to care the slightest bit that he was blocking traffic and making people mad at him. "You got your cell phone?"

"Duh," replied Billy rudely.

But James wasn't listening anymore. He was text messaging his friend again. "All right, all right! I heard you!" he yelled out the window to the people in the cars behind him. "Take a chill pill!"

There were dozens of trees and shrubs and miles of grassy lawn at the park, and it all looked like it had just come from Mr. O'Malley's barbershop at the train station. Everything was trimmed and neat. There wasn't a single twig out of place.

"Isn't this the greatest?" said Billy like he had died and gone to heaven. "Everyone back at school is stuck doing math with Mr. Hervey, and here we are in the park!"

Callum had the strangest feeling that he was in the wrong place all of a sudden. He didn't know exactly why. Would he have been happier back at school, stuck doing math with Mr. Hervey? If so, how come? Maybe he was simply curious about what the other kids were up to. For all he knew, math might be just as fun as being in the park. Could you do math outdoors?

"Let's play a game," said Billy. "I'll race you to that tree and back. Nah. I don't want to race. I know! Let's play Army. I'll be the good guy. You be the enemy. We'll each occupy one of those banks of shrubs up on the hill on either side of the footpath and then we'll reconnoiter and I'll pretend to blow your brains out."

Oh! thought Callum. This sounds familiar. Dad and Uncle Rick had pretended to kill each other all the time. The only thing that had stopped Dad from actually killing Uncle Rick was probably the fact that it was more fun to be an Alpha when there was a Beta around to remind you of how important you were.

"Okay, here's the plan," said Billy, putting his arm around Callum's shoulders. "You go to your territory, I'll go to mine, and then we'll both count to ten and start to reconnoiter. But it's hand weapons only, all right? No grenades or rocket launchers. Agreed?"

"Agreed," answered Callum. He didn't even bother to ask what a grenade or a rocket launcher was.

Billy went off to the bank of shrubs on one side of the footpath, and Callum went off to his bank of shrubs on the hill at the other side. Then he counted to ten and started to reconnoiter, which in this case meant spying on the enemy without being seen.

He thought back to all he had learned about hunting from the pack. The wolves usually tried to chase their quarry until it was ready to fall over in utter exhaustion, but he didn't want to reveal his presence to his prey. Quickly, quietly, and very cautiously, he slunk from bush to bush, and then darted behind a tree, and then hid behind a bush again, and then caught sight of Billy trying not very successfully to hide behind a different bush up ahead. Billy's back was turned, and he had a big rock in his hand for some reason.

Callum prepared to attack. Hand weapons only, Billy had said. Did that mean using your razor-sharp teeth wasn't allowed? He decided that he would simply attempt to overpower Billy and hold him against the ground like Dad did to Uncle Rick.

Whether from the army's perspective or a predator's point of view, Billy could have used a few lessons in warding off an attack. He wasn't watching his back at all. Callum pounced, and Billy went down like a sack of old potatoes. The rock in his hand flew off into the bushes.

"Ow!" he cried. "Not so hard! I give up, I give up!"

Callum loosened his grip a notch or two. Clearly he had overestimated the enemy's forces. He couldn't help but feel a little let down. When challenging an Alpha, you should feel lucky to escape with your life, not hold him down easy-peasy.

"Ow, ow!" cried Billy again. "You're hurting me! What part of 'I give up' don't you understand?"

Yes, it was humiliating for a Beta to let go of an Alpha first, when it should have been the other way around. It should have been even more humiliating for the Alpha. But when Billy got to his feet he seemed happy enough.

Not so happy as to want to play the same game over again, however.

"That's enough of that," he said, all out of breath. "Man,

you kicked my butt! Actually, I was expecting you to shoot me from a distance, not go all commando on me like that. Go on. Tell me. Where'd you learn those moves? Karate class?"

"I just imagined that I was the predator and you were the prey," said Callum sensibly. They were two of the words that he had always been sure of.

"Predator and prey," repeated Billy in absolute awe. "Holy moly! I've never played that one before. Cool! It sounds fun. Let's play that! Only let's *both* be predators this time."

Callum was a little confused. That's not the way it worked in the Wild. Predators never hunted each other. Somebody had to be the prey. He tried to explain that to Billy.

"Don't sweat it," Billy said. "Look around. There's plenty of prey to take down. Unsuspecting prey, that is. See?"

He pointed to the footpath ahead, where a woman was headed in their direction, pushing a baby carriage.

"How's that for prey?" he said. "Here, let's lie in wait."

He pulled Callum behind a bush near the footpath.

"Don't make a sound," he instructed, sounding Alpha-like again, to Callum's relief. "We want to take our prey by the utmost surprise."

They both held their breath. Gradually the woman walked up to them. Through a break in the bushes Callum saw she was smiling, and he could hear a gentle snatch of song as she hummed an aimless melody to herself and her baby.

"Look at her," whispered Billy. "She doesn't suspect a thing. Wait for my signal, and then we'll both jump out and bring her down."

Callum was about to tell him that predators usually gave their prey a fighting chance to run for their lives, and it didn't seem likely that this one could run very far or even at all given the baby carriage that she was pushing, but before he could get a word out Billy yelled, "*Now!*" and jumped through the bushes, and he instinctively joined the hunt.

Together they rushed at the unsuspecting victim, snarling like crazy and altogether coming off as vicious, bloodthirsty killers.

"Blankety-blank!" exclaimed the poor frightened woman, holding her hand to her throat. She had stopped the baby carriage with such a sudden jolt that the baby inside it began to cry.

"Look what you've done!" she said worriedly and then took her baby out of the carriage and held it close to soothe it. "There, there," she said softly until it stopped crying, and then she scolded her attackers.

"What in the name of all that is good and decent in this world do you think you're doing, jumping out of the bushes and scaring innocent people nearly to death?" she demanded.

"Hey, did you hear that?" Billy said to Callum excitedly. "We scared her nearly to death! We just have to leap out a little faster next time, and snarl a little more ferociously."

"I have never seen such irresponsible behavior or met two more mean-spirited and inconsiderate boys in all my life," reprimanded the frightened woman. "It's troublemakers like you that give private schools a bad name. Where are your parents, for goodness' sake?"

"My parents are in the South of France," replied Billy.

"My parents are somewhere in the woods," answered Callum. "At least, I *think* they're my parents."

"That is just sad," said the woman, shaking her head pityingly. She put her baby back in the carriage and continued down the footpath, still shaking her head.

Callum and Billy stood for a moment without saying anything.

Then Billy said, "Holy moly, we really freaked her out. That was fun, wasn't it? Let's do it again. But let's go over there this time, on the other side of the fountain."

Callum didn't think it was such a good idea to play this game again after what had happened with the woman and her baby. In fact, it seemed kind of crazy to do it a second time. But Billy raced ahead, laughing his head off in eager anticipation of another awful thrill.

Callum was concerned. Billy certainly seemed to be falling short of what an Alpha Male should be. Alphas liked to have fun, to be sure, but only in the right time and place, and it wasn't very often that they'd do something crazy. Still, the Beta rules held strong, and so he followed Billy to the bushes on the other side of the fountain.

The fountain was an elaborate circular marble affair, with statues of fishes and birds and whatnot plastered all over it.

"Hold on," Callum told Billy and stopped to take a drink. He simply knelt on the wide marble edge and stuck his face into the bubbling brown water.

"Man," said Billy admiringly, although a little grossed out. "You are *so* hard-core. That water is disgusting. It's got duck poop in it!"

As if in agreement, half a dozen ducks paddled by and looked at him funny.

Callum didn't mind, but truth be told, the water did taste bad, not like the clear mountain streams he was used to. He was pretty sure that he'd never drink from a fountain that had duck poop in it again.

"Over here!" Billy said and hid behind the biggest, thickest bush he could find.

Callum went and joined him there. The bush was so dense that there were no breaks in it to look through, but they could hear if anyone was coming down the footpath.

"Shhh," said Billy. "Listen!"

Sure enough, they heard the sound of footsteps on the gravel.

"Wait for my signal," said Billy again. "Then leap out like you mean it this time."

Callum wondered if Mr. Hervey was done with math yet back at the Hargrove Academy for the Gifted, Bright, and

Perceptive Child. He tried to remember what Lila had told him. What came after math? Some sort of science. That sounded interesting too. He really didn't understand yet why Billy Bankson thought it was more fun being at the park instead of at school. It seemed that Billy had gotten things mixed up somehow.

"*Now!*" Billy shouted, and without giving it another thought Callum leaped out from the bushes to attack whatever unsuspecting victim had wandered into their clutches this time.

"*Ha! Got you!*" said a big, burly man in a dark blue uniform with a silver badge on the chest. He caught Callum by the wrist with one hand and Billy by the wrist with the other. "I've had a serious complaint about the two of you," he said gruffly, "and so I thought I'd come by to see what you were up to myself."

"Let go!" cried Billy. "You're hurting me! I didn't do anything. It was all *his* idea."

Callum didn't like this one bit. In the Wild, an Alpha never blamed a Beta for anything. He didn't like seeing another police officer either, after his encounter with the one who had called the dogcatcher on the street that morning. But there wasn't anything he could do about it, since a hand that felt like a solid metal clamp was wrapped around his wrist.

"Didn't do anything, eh?" said the big, burly police officer. "Other than jump out from the bushes and try to scare an innocent lady right out of her skin, you mean. And her with a baby barely ten months old! Do you think that's proper park behavior? Because I'm here to tell you right now that it ain't."

CHAPTER THIRTEEN
Callum at a Sleepover

I hope you guys know how lucky you are to be let off with just a warning," said James when Billy and Callum were safely riding in the long, sleek black car once again.

"The police could have locked you up and thrown away the key," he went on with a shudder. "And believe me, it takes a strong person to survive a jail sentence. Even the wildest and most ferocious animals get their spirits broken when they're put inside a cage. I'd rather have my lungs ripped out through my throat than be stuck behind bars."

"Aw, it wasn't that big a deal," said Billy, shrugging it off. "What could they do to us? We're kids."

"Oh yeah?" said James. "In some countries, kids like you get locked up for doing a lot less than what you and your friend pulled today, and they throw away the key and let 'em rot."

Billy was silent at that. Callum counted his blessings that

the police officer let them go and didn't call the pound or wherever it was that they locked people up and then threw away the key. In many respects it seemed to be a lot easier to survive in the Wild than in the city. He wondered if Mom and Dad and Aunt Trudy and Uncle Rick and Grampa had gotten the moose that they went after. He hoped Aunt Trudy had survived another kick in the head if they did.

"Where to now?" James asked Billy. "Are we dropping your friend off somewhere?"

"Nah," said Billy. "He's coming home with me." Then he said to Callum, "We'll have a sleepover. You can call your parents from my place to get permission."

"I don't need my parents' permission," said Callum. He couldn't contact the pack even if he wanted to, he thought sadly. From here on out they were only a memory, doomed to fade as time went by until they were as dim and distant as the shadowy figures at the back of his mind, the ones he was so mad at. Furious, really.

"You are *so totally* hard-core," said Billy admiringly. "Have I told you that before?"

Callum certainly needed to find a proper den in which to spend the night. Billy's was as good as any. Still, he wished he had more of a choice. Hanging out with Billy wasn't as rewarding as he thought it would be. James dropped them off in front of an enormous brick building with different-colored flags flying in front. *Honk! Honk! Honk!* went the car behind them.

"Try to stay out of trouble for at least an hour or two, okay, pal?" he said to Billy. "And you too, kid," he told Callum. Then he yelled out the window, "Hold onto your hat, why don't you?" and pulled out his cell phone and began text messaging his friend again.

They took an elevator ride to get to Billy's den. It was the scariest thing Callum had experienced since the train began to move the other morning. And it was weirder than that, even. By the time he got out, he was sweaty and shaking all over.

"Relax, will you?" said Billy. "I told you, my parents aren't home. They hardly ever are."

The elevator had brought them directly to the den. It wasn't a very cozy den. It was too big for that. There was a lot of furniture grouped here and there, but mostly it was open space. All in all, it looked like a parking lot with a roof over it.

"Billy, is that you?" came a frantic-sounding voice from the kitchen.

A frizzy-haired woman wearing an apron that had pictures of forks and knives on it came rushing toward them like a hungry hawk swooping down on a couple of chipmunks.

The room was so big that, as fast as she was going, it still took her a while to reach them.

Close up, Callum could see how frizzy her hair was. Really frizzy.

"James told me that he picked you up at the police station," she said anxiously. "What did they want with my poor little Billy-Willy? Don't tell me! You would never break the law. You're honest, polite, and you care about people."

Man, does she have the wrong guy in mind, thought Callum.

"It wasn't my fault," said her poor little Billy-Willy, sounding especially poor and little. "I didn't do what they said I did."

"Shush," said the frizzy-haired woman. "Of course not. You're cooperative, friendly, and dependable. You're also conscientious and giving."

She bit her lower lip, not from emotion but because it seemed that she was concentrating on something like crazy, and held out her arms for a hug. In one of her hands was an open book.

Billy ignored her open arms, but he didn't ignore the book.

"Oh, great," he said contemptuously. "What are you reading this time?"

"This is the latest breakthrough in child psychology, Billy, honey," said the frizzy-haired woman. "It's called *Dealing With the Troubled Child*, and I'm learning all about positive reinforcement and the power of suggestion. Thank you for asking about it. You've got such an inquisitive mind. You're sensitive, insightful, and you have a knack for solving complicated problems."

She turned to Callum with an accusing look in her eyes.

"And who are *you*?" she demanded. "Are you the one who got my Billy in trouble?"

"I'm Clam," said Callum. "Like the mollusk. And we both got in trouble."

"Frieda, leave him alone," said Billy. "He can't help it. He wasn't raised right. He had a bad home environment."

"Why, you poor thing," the frizzy-haired woman said supportively, changing her tune. She took Callum's hand and squeezed it tightly. "You be strong, you hear?" she said. "You can be anything you want to be, if you only apply yourself. Rethink your life choices. It's never too late to make a change for the better."

Callum was reminded of how crazy Aunt Trudy had acted the time she accidentally ate some poison berries. Maybe this frizzy-haired woman had eaten some poison berries too. She certainly acted like it.

"Wash up, you two," she said, suddenly looking and sounding as worn out as if she had just run for miles. "Dinner's nearly ready."

"I want to order a pizza," declared Billy.

"But Billy, dear," said Frieda with a smile, although Callum could tell that she was also gritting her teeth. "I've made three-cheese lasagna, your favorite."

"I don't care," said Billy inconsiderately. "I want pizza."

"Very well," Frieda said, still smiling and gritting away. "Do you want to call the pizza parlor, or shall I?"

"You call," said Billy. "We're gonna go play. Get the number seven, the Meat Eater's Delight. Extra large. And tell them to bring a six-pack of cherry colas while they're at it."

"Whatever you say. You're compassionate, you're helpful, and you have a loving demeanor, Billy-Willy," said Frieda with a concentrated effort, clutching her psychology book like it was a life preserver and she was adrift in stormy seas, and then ran off to call up the pizza parlor.

"Frieda can be such a drag," complained Billy before she was even out of earshot. "But her heart is in the right place. She lets me do whatever I want. Come on. Let's go to my room."

He led Callum through the vast open area past couches and chairs and tables and desks and tall leafy plants in big copper pots. Finally they reached a separate room where the walls were covered with bookshelves. Each of the shelves was crammed to the gills with toys and sports equipment, every kind you can imagine and then some. And it all looked brand new, as if it hadn't been touched.

"Cool," said Callum, who had never seen so much stuff in his life. He didn't know what all the various types of balls and bats were for, but every last one of them looked totally fun.

"What's cool?" asked Billy. "Oh, that! I keep telling Frieda to throw that stuff out. She just tells me I'm lucky to have it. I think she's crazy. Who needs a bunch of junk?"

It didn't look like junk to Callum. He looked at Billy, and it occurred to him that Frieda wasn't the only one around this den with a screw loose.

"Listen to this," Billy said and tapped a few keys on the computer that lay on the floor near his messy, unmade bed. "Here," he said, tossing a bunch of empty snack containers out of the way. "Sit down."

Callum sat down on the floor, and all of a sudden a deafening noise blasted from two mammoth speakers on either side of Billy's bed.

The noise was so loud that it made Callum want to run and hide. If he had been outside, he would have tried to dig a hole and bury his head in the ground.

"*This is my favorite song,*" Billy yelled in order to be heard above the din. "*What do you think of it? Pretty sweet, huh?*"

Callum couldn't have answered even if he had understood what Billy was talking about. The frightening noise had pushed every last thought from his brain.

"*Here,*" yelled Billy, pointing to the computer screen. "*Watch the video that goes with it. It rocks!*"

Callum looked at the moving images on the glowing screen. A scary hooded figure in a terrifying mask was stalking prey in a manner that clearly had nothing to do with dinner or the need to support any pack. The prey he was stalking was other people, which didn't seem right, and he was hacking them to pieces with a big jagged knife.

"*Isn't that great?*" yelled Billy. "*It's from a movie. I really want to see it, but it's rated R. I'm going to get James to sneak me into the theater this weekend. Want to come along?"*

Callum didn't know what an R-rated movie was, but if it was anything like what he was watching on Billy's computer screen, he didn't want to have anything to do with it. In fact, he wanted to run away from it as fast as he could.

"*Billy, dear,*" Frieda yelled, poking her head around the corner of one of the toy-crammed bookshelves, "turn that thing off, sweetheart. Your dad's on the phone, precious."

"*What did she say?*" Billy yelled at Callum.

"Billy, darling, sweetheart, dearest, I said *turn that thing off,*" Frieda yelled with a definite tone of irritation in her voice.

"*Just ignore her,*" Billy yelled at Callum. "*She'll go away.*"

"*She says you should turn that thing off,*" yelled Callum.

"*What did you say?*" yelled Billy. "*Wait. I'll turn this thing off.*"

He tapped a few keys on the computer and the terrible noise disappeared, leaving a throbbing feeling deep inside Callum's ears.

"What do you want, Frieda?" Billy demanded in a surly manner. "You know better than to bug me when I'm playing with my friends."

"I've come to tell you that your dad's on the phone, Billy, darling," said Frieda in a gentler tone, relieved beyond measure that the racket had stopped. "Isn't that exciting? Your dad is actually taking time out of his busy schedule to talk to you."

"What does he want?" asked Billy suspiciously. "What did you tell him about the police station?"

"Why, nothing, Billy, dear," said Frieda. "If anything, I told him you were intelligent, persevering, and generous."

"So then why is he calling?" asked Billy. "It's not my birthday or anything."

"You can ask him yourself, dearest," said Frieda, holding out the phone in a way that was somewhat demanding.

"All right, all right," Billy consented grudgingly. "Hi, Dad. What's up? Yeah, I've been really busy at school. We had a math test today with Mr. Hervey. I got a Satisfactory. Yeah, it was no real surprise, with all the studying I've been doing and all. The football? Yeah, I got it. Me and my friends played with it all afternoon after school. It was neat."

Boy, thought Callum, has Billy got his dad fooled too.

"Okay, Dad," said Billy. "Thanks for calling. Tell Mom I said hi. Bye."

He handed the phone to the frizzy-haired woman. "There, now," Frieda said approvingly. "That wasn't so hard, was it? Your pizza's here. It's a Meat Eater's Delight, extra large, just like you wanted. I've set the table."

"Bring it in here," said Billy. "We'll eat it right out of the box."

Again it seemed like Frieda was concentrating on something so much that it caused every muscle in her body to seize up. "Are you sure about that, dear?" she said sweetly, although clenching her fists. "It's so much easier to sit at the table."

"Frieda, are you deaf or something?" Billy retorted rudely. "Didn't you hear what I said?"

"Positive reinforcement and the power of suggestion," Frieda muttered under her breath, then said sweetly, "Of course I heard you, Billy, darling. You're easygoing, frank, and dutiful. You didn't tell me you got a Satisfactory on your math test today. Congratulations, sweetie."

There must be a whole lot of poison berries around here somewhere, thought Callum when she'd gone off to get the pizza. There better not be any on the pizza, whatever pizza was.

Frieda returned in a jiff with the box of pizza, the six-pack of cherry colas, and some paper napkins, handed it to Billy, and then hurried away as if she couldn't get back to the kitchen fast enough. Billy threw the whole lot on the floor, where it came to rest atop a pile of old soda cans, dirty socks, and Whing Dings wrappers, and then devoted his full attention to cramming as much pizza into his mouth as it could hold.

"Oh, it's hot!" he cried frantically, still going strong. "It's burning the skin off the roof of my mouth!"

Callum was impressed. Even Dad at his greediest had never devoured food as voraciously as that. As for the pizza, it was the most surprising thing all day. He remembered pizza! He had eaten it before, although he couldn't remember where or when. It was the most delicious thing he had ever tasted, not counting cherry cola, but then he had thought the same thing about everything he had eaten since he'd gotten on the train that morning. City food almost made up for the hassle of city life, he decided.

"Man, I'm stuffed," Billy said finally, and Callum could believe it. Billy tossed the empty pizza box into a pile of trash in the corner and then threw himself facedown on the bed. A minute later he was making loud snoring sounds, just like Dad used to do.

Okay, thought Callum, in some ways Billy *was* an Alpha Male after all. But there was more to being an Alpha than just stuffing your face full of food and snoring.

He tried to make himself fall asleep, but couldn't force his way into dreamland. He thought about Lila. She could probably have taught him everything he needed to know about survival in the city, just by example. He would like to meet her pack sometime. They must be very strong to have produced such an Alpha Female in a cub so young. She had a knack for making Omegas feel important, which was nice of her. She would have liked Grampa, probably. And Grampa would have certainly liked her. To gnaw on, at least.

Before falling into a fitful, short-lived sleep, Callum decided he had made a mistake. He should have followed Lila home, not Billy Bankson.

CHAPTER FOURTEEN

Callum in the Park Again

Callum woke in the dark in Billy Bankson's bedroom. His top half was lying next to Billy on Billy's messy bed, and his bottom half was hanging off it, with his feet resting on a pile of trash in the corner.

All was quiet. Billy had stopped snoring, although every now and then he made a weird snorting sound or said something in his sleep that sounded like, "It wasn't me. I didn't do it!"

With nothing to distract him, Callum could really tell how much Billy's space smelled like dirty clothes and garbage. It was the messiest den he could have imagined, a real disgrace to dens everywhere. Even Grampa, who loved things that were disgusting and gross, would have turned up his nose at it. He thought of getting up and moving to one of the couches in the big, open area outside Billy's bedroom, but then he decided that what he really wanted was a breath of fresh air, and for that he would have to go outside.

He got up and went downstairs in the elevator, which wasn't so bad now that he knew what to expect. Outside, the night air was crisp and clean. The sky was clear and dark. He felt a hundred times better. A few stars twinkled here and there, and a full moon was on the rise. Without really thinking about it, he began to walk toward the park.

It was cold, but not any colder than he was used to in the woods. His Hargrove blazer kept him warm, and the walk made him warmer still.

As he turned the corner, he saw a couple of stray dogs quietly tipping over a trash can. Messy garbage spilled out onto the sidewalk, but they cleaned it up as best they could, he was happy to see. Obviously, they had paid close attention to the advice he had given them earlier. They narrowed their eyes and bared their teeth as he approached, and then they seemed to recognize him and smiled and wagged their tails. Callum smiled back, and once again he felt the disappointing absence of a tail on his backside.

"Stay," he instructed them with a low growling bark, but he wouldn't have minded if they disobeyed him and followed him instead. It was a dangerous thing to be outside the den in the middle of the night.

"Never leave the den at night," Grampa had warned him more than once. "Not even if you need to squat under a bush to relieve yourself. Just hold it in and pray for daylight. There are some mean and deadly animals out there in the dark. Meaner and deadlier than you can ever imagine, with your puny brain."

And yet here he was alone on the street after midnight. It only served to show his sorry state of mind. Just the other night he was safely tucked between Mom and Aunt Trudy, and Dad was staring at him like he wanted to devour him. But now that part of his life had come to a close, like a poem that had reached its final rhyme, and he felt lost and alone.

Somehow, some way, he had to fit in with his own kind, and finding his place in this strange new world was going to be trickier than he thought, especially when appearances could be so deceiving. At first glance, Billy Bankson looked like true Alpha material, but the more you looked, the more you saw that he didn't even qualify as a Beta. Uncle Rick would have mopped the floor with him, and Uncle Rick was as Beta as Beta could be.

I'm *fierce*, Callum reminded himself for the billionth time. I'm *savage*. I am a *wild thing*! But he didn't have the courage to bare his teeth or make his hands look like deadly claws. And anyway, there was no one to see it if he did.

By this time, he had reached the park. It appeared a lot more like wilderness in the moonlight than it had in the light of day. Callum was reminded of the woods and its impression of Nature's mystery and the possibility of hidden danger in its untold depths.

A little breeze stirred the leaves. The trees seemed to be talking to one another.

That's a language I will *never* understand, Callum thought sadly.

He felt invisible, as if he were only a part of the breeze. The gravel didn't even crunch beneath his feet.

Although the park seemed so still, he knew from experience how much activity lay hidden just beneath its surface. Underneath the grass, hungry moles were tunneling in search of juicy earthworms to eat. They were so far underground that they probably didn't know or care if it was day or night. Agile opossums were prowling in the treetops overhead, looking to rob sleepy birds of the eggs in their nests. All of the other nocturnal animals were busy too, getting their chores done and making their ways in the world, unseen. They had probably grown up in the park and didn't know that any other place existed. They were lucky that they didn't have to start learning to live their lives over from scratch with a whole new set of rules.

Not that Callum really regretted leaving the den. He knew that he had been pretty useless to the pack. If Mom hadn't wanted him around to be her Salty Lollipop, it was a good bet that the others would have devoured him long ago.

Hopefully he had more to offer among his own kind. If it turned out that he could actually contribute something for once, all of his fear and confusion would be worth it.

And at least no one was licking his cheek off with a sandpaper tongue.

He suddenly glimpsed a flickering light up ahead in the

darkness, and his sensitive ears caught a blur of soft voices. He was more careful than ever not to make a sound as he crept forward to see who was there.

The light came from a fire crackling inside a big metal drum.

Callum hadn't smelled the smoke earlier because the breeze was carrying it in the opposite direction. He smelled it now, though. It was the same kind of smell that had caused Aunt Trudy to worry herself half to death when she detected it on Callum's borrowed clothes back at the den, what he had imagined she said came from a campfire.

So this is a campfire, he thought, and all at once his mind seemed to be crammed with strong thoughts and his heart spilled over with strong emotions, and for a moment he didn't know what to do or to think. All he could remember was the terrible time long ago when he felt so lonely and scared that he thought he was the only living thing in the whole of Creation. But the campfire didn't scare him. Even from so far away he could sense the warmth that it brought to the chilly night air.

Three raggedy old men were grouped around the fire, warming their faces and hands. They reminded Callum of Grampa with their saggy, faded-looking eyes, and the same sort of bristly gray hair as Grampa's sprouted from their pointy chins. Raggedy knit hats were pulled around their heads. The thin coats hanging from their bony shoulders were raggedy too, and their shoes had holes in the places where the flimsy leather wasn't held together by string and tape.

One of them was tall, one was short, and one was in-between.

"Really nice night," Callum heard the tall Grampa say.

"The nicest one all week," said the short one.

"Not like the night before last," added the one in between.

"Nothing like it," said the tall one. "I can't take that rain."

"Neither can I," said the short one. "It soaks me to the skin."

"I don't mind it," said the one in between. "It makes everything clean and fresh. It's the cold I can't stand."

"Well, we've got a fire now, boys," said the tall one. "For as long as it lasts, anyway. Let's soak up as much of its warm, golden energy as we can hold. It feels like melted butter on popcorn to me."

"It feels like I'm being hugged by a sunbeam," said the short one.

"I feel like a scrambled egg in a frying pan," said the one in between, who was getting too close to the flames. "Ouch!"

Just then, Callum lost his balance. His foot landed hard on a big, dry stick, and the snap that it made as it broke sounded like a gun going off in the still night air.

The three Grampas were shocked into silence.

Callum froze too.

Nobody made a move or a sound. All that could be heard

was the fire as it crackled and popped. Then the tall Grampa said, "What in blazes was that?" very low under his breath.

"Maybe it's a raccoon, or a possum," said the short one. "Unless it's something meaner and more deadly."

"It sounded pretty big to me," said the one in between. "And it sounded hungry too."

"You think everything's hungry," said the tall one, "just because you are. All the same, I hope it's not something that wants to eat us."

"It better not be," said the short one. "I don't have any meat on my bones to spare."

"One of you go take a look," said the one in between. "And see if the coast is clear."

"I'm not afraid," said the tall one. "I'm happy to do anything as long as I'm not getting soaked to the skin."

He picked up the long pointed stick that he had been poking the fire with and approached the bush where Callum was hiding.

"Here, little raccoon!" he called, trying to sound happy and fun, although Callum could tell that he was pretty much scared half to death. "Here, little possum!"

As if! Callum thought. He liked raccoons and opossums well enough, but he didn't like being mistaken for one.

"Here, little whatever you are," the tall Grampa called, nervously poking the long pointed stick in the bushes. "Good, sweet, kind little whatever you are."

The stick suddenly hit something fleshy.

"Ouch!" cried Callum, and the tall Grampa hightailed it back to the campfire as quick as could be.

"Jumping Jehoshaphat!" he cried.

All three Grampas grouped themselves together in military fashion and faced the bush Callum was hiding in. "Don't try to attack us!" said the short one bravely. "I'm warning you for your own safety. I'm an ex-Marine, and I've seen combat. I can break a man in two with my fists!"

"I was in the Army Reserve!" said the one in between. "I can break a man in half with one hand!"

"I've got a pointed stick!" said the tall one. "And I'm not afraid to poke a man to death with it. Come out with your hands up!"

Callum thought it over. There wasn't much else he could do but surrender. Truth be told, he really wanted to warm himself by the fire. It looked like a fun thing to do, as well as cozy. He slowly stepped away from the bushes with his hands in the air.

"Good man," said the short Grampa. "You don't want to face my fists of fury."

"Will you look at that?" said the one in between. "It's just a cub."

"Come on and warm yourself by the fire, buddy," said the tall one. "Don't be afraid. There are some mean and deadly people roaming the city at night, but we aren't them. Here. Take my pointed stick. If you think any of us is about to do you any harm, why, you can take this stick and poke out his eye with it."

"What makes you think that we're not the ones who are in danger, Tom?" the short Grampa asked the tall one. "I think all of us should have a pointed stick."

"So go get one, Dick," the tall one replied. "Nobody's stopping you. But if you ask me, this guy looks all right. You're all right, aren't you, buddy?" he said to Callum. "What's your name?"

"Clam Firehead," said Callum. "Like the mollusk."

"Do I like mollusks?" said the tall one, licking his thin gray lips hungrily. "You bet I do! Yum! My name is Tom. Nice to meet you."

"Firehead?" said the short one. "You got that right. Just look at your bright red hair! I feel like I could warm my hands over your noggin, same as I'm doing over the fire in this oil drum. My name is Dick. The pleasure is mine."

"Don't mind him," the one in between said to Callum. "Someone dropped him on his head when he was a baby. I'm Harry. I'm the smart one in this bunch. Welcome to our motley crew." Then he said to the tall Grampa, "You'd better take care, Tom. He's got the pointed stick."

"You can have it back, if you want," said Callum to Tom.

"Nonsense," Tom replied. "Go ahead and poke the fire with it. It could use some poking, seems to me."

Callum poked the fire with the long pointed stick, and the flames rose up as high as could be. Everyone was silent for a minute or two, intent on simply basking in its warmth and cheerful glow.

"I'll wager someone's looking for you, Clam," Harry

finally spoke up. "Shouldn't you let them know where you are? We can walk you out of here in a group for safety's sake, if you'd like us to, and you can give them a call."

"No one's looking for me," said Callum. "I'm all alone in the world. I have nowhere to go."

"I know what you mean," said Dick. "It sure feels like that sometimes, even if it isn't true."

"But you go to school don't you?" asked Harry, looking at his blazer.

"I just went for one day," said Callum. "I didn't even make it till math."

"I dropped out of school too," said Tom. "Biggest mistake of my life. Or at least one of them."

"Not to be rude or anything," said Dick to Callum, "but you didn't happen to bring any food with you, did you? A candy bar, perhaps? Or a couple of cookies?"

All three Grampas looked at Callum hopefully.

"No, sorry, I didn't," said Callum.

He thought about Billy Bankson stuffing his face full of pizza. Billy had eaten enough that night for three or four people at least. And he had ignored the three-cheese lasagna, which was supposed to be his favorite.

Maybe Callum could go back and get the lasagna. But he imagined Frieda would probably have a heart attack if he tried to give Billy's favorite three-cheese lasagna to three raggedy Grampas in the park.

"Do you have a breath mint, at least?" asked Tom.

Again, all three Grampas looked at Callum with hope in their eyes.

"No, I'm sorry," he said regretfully. Billy probably had tons of those too, whatever they were.

"That's a shame," said Tom.

"Oh, well," said Harry, "I guess we'll just have to live with old Dragon Breath here a little longer."

"I brushed my teeth three months ago," protested Dick. "Which is more than the two of you can say."

"Where are our manners, gentlemen?" Harry said to the others. "We haven't explained ourselves properly."

He turned to Callum and said, "We are the Forgotten Men. Not all of them, mind you, just three good examples. Nobody wants us. We have no families, no jobs, no money, and no food. We've only got each other, Mother Nature, and this beautiful public park to hang out in. And I'm gratified to tell you that on rare, special occasions like meeting you tonight, what we have seems more than enough and we couldn't be happier."

"I could be happier," disagreed Tom. "With a twelve-ounce steak and a nice comfy bed to sleep in."

"I could be happier too," said Dick. "With a cherry cola and a hot-fudge sundae."

I love cherry cola too, Callum thought automatically, although too much of it made him feel like he was about to explode.

"Yes," Harry went on, "this park is a place of many

delights for us. We can visit the arboretum anytime we want to, and we can look over the fence and see the animals in the zoo."

"Not all of them," complained Tom.

"I'm just saying," said Harry, "that there's one thing that no one can take away from us, and that's our ability to count our blessings. We can thank the Great Spirit for all the things we have, not blame Her for all the things we don't have."

"And we can always ask Her for a little more," said Tom.

"Not that it does any good," said Dick.

Callum nodded in agreement, glad that these guys knew about the Great Spirit, same as he did.

Just then came the sound of twigs snapping again in the bushes, but this time Callum had nothing to do with it.

"Great day in the morning!" cried Tom, hurriedly looking around for another pointed stick. "What is it now?"

"It's the long arm of the law come to apprehend you three criminals!" said a stern voice from the bushes, and out stepped the same burly police officer that had apprehended Billy and Callum in the park that afternoon.

Callum quickly moved behind Harry so as not to be seen.

"Have a heart, officer," said Dick. "It's freezing out here tonight. We need our little bun warmer."

"No can do," said the police officer gruffly. "This is an illegal campfire. And no one is allowed in the park after midnight. You know the rules. But just to show that I'm not a bad guy, I've got vouchers for the three of you to stay in the city shelter tonight."

"I can't breathe at the city shelter!" complained Tom. "It smells like old socks in there, and I get enough of that as it is. I need fresh air!"

"I wasn't asking if you *wanted* to go," said the police officer. "I was *telling* you to. Let's get a move on. Throw some dirt on that fire, and get your butts in gear."

An eerie howling in the distance suddenly broke the still of the night, a single voice that was quickly joined by another and then another until there was a whole chorus of high, wavering cries.

Oh-whooooooo . . .

OWWW-hoooooo . . .

OHHH-whhhhhooOOO . . .

"What's *that?*" asked the police officer nervously. He didn't come to the park in the middle of the night very often, only when he had nothing better to do. "Where's it coming from?" he asked the three Grampas shakily.

"It's coming from the zoo, of course," said Tom. "The animals are restless. Who can blame them? It's a full moon tonight, after all. The lunar pull is pretty irresistible. We should all be howling. I know I want to."

"I want to too," said Dick.

"Count me in on that," said Harry.

"Enough with the yakking," said the police officer, who was more eager than ever to get a move on. "Off we go. We'll never get to the city shelter at this rate."

"What about our little friend here?" said Harry.

"What little friend?" asked the police officer.

"Why, Clam Firehead, of course!" said the three Grampas at once. "Like the mollusk! Yum!"

"Not the kid with the kooky name again!" said the police officer. "What's he doing here at this time of night?"

All four men turned to look for him, but Callum was gone.

He had heard the howling too, and had already hurried off in the direction it was coming from.

CHAPTER FIFTEEN
Lila Goes Online

By the end of school that day, Lila was in a terrible mood, the kind her dad called "a real funk" and Charlie the cabbie called "the sulky sulks."

Charlie arrived in the lineup right on time, as always. Lila and Stanley got in the back, and Lila slammed the door shut, which was something that she never did usually.

"Careful," said Charlie. "Don't break it. It's only reinforced steel, you know."

"*Sorry,*" said Lila too loudly.

"Aren't we missing someone?" asked Charlie. "The cab feels a little lighter than it did this morning."

"It's C-c-clam," stammered Stanley helpfully. "C-c-clam isn't here."

"Clam's not c-c-coming," said Lila, mocking Stanley's stammer, which was an incredibly rude thing to do and something that she had never done before and hopefully would never do again.

"Hey!" said Charlie sternly. "None of that behavior in my cab!"

"I'm sorry, Stanley," said Lila sincerely. "I didn't mean it."

"That's okay," said Stanley, who was extremely understanding, especially where students in the Yellow Level were concerned. "I forgive you."

"I'm sorry, Charlie," said Lila. "I really am. It won't happen again."

"That's better," said Charlie. "I'm surprised at you, Lila. What on earth happened today that gave you the sulky sulks?"

Lila was at a loss for words, although she knew what the problem was.

It was Clam, of course.

He had skipped school after lunch with that horrible Billy Bankson, and so he'd missed out on math with Mr. Hervey and then life sciences, where Mr. Sears had shown a fascinating film about the life of the giant squid.

Ordinarily, after watching a fascinating film about the life of the giant squid, Lila would be as happy and excited as if it were her birthday and the holidays all rolled into one. That's how much she liked learning about animals. She was planning on becoming a veterinarian when she grew up and hoped to successfully operate on a wounded giant squid one day and then release it back into the Wild.

And that wasn't all. After the film, Mr. Sears had

announced an upcoming field trip to the zoo in the park, which ordinarily would have sent her over the moon.

But instead, she felt hurt and let down. And she was confused by it.

Why should she care if a boy she hardly knew decided to run off and set a bad example? Why did she take it so personally? Was it because Clam had the exact same shade of bright red hair as she did? If so, why was that so important?

"Why isn't he here then?" asked Charlie, sounding a little hurt himself. "Did he get a ride home with some other cab driver?"

Lila knew it wasn't right to rat on other people's bad behavior when it had nothing to do with her. The important exception was if danger of any kind was involved. Then you had to rat, no matter who might get in trouble, because keeping people safe from danger was absolutely crucial.

It didn't seem very dangerous for Clam to have run off with Billy, but she couldn't stop herself from ratting on him anyway.

"He ran off with Billy Bankson," she told Charlie in a rush of emotion. "They skipped school together after lunch."

"Billy Bankson?" said Charlie. "Oh, brother. That guy gets into more trouble than any other boy I ever heard of. He needs somebody to straighten him out but good, although it would probably take the whole U.S. Army to do a job as big as that, am I right? I'm not surprised they ran off together, though. Didn't I hear that he and Clam were already friends?"

"I thought so this morning," said Lila. "But it didn't seem like Clam even knew who Billy was until Billy stole a pudding from Teddy Thompson during lunch. Then he went right over to Billy's table and made friends with him. I saw it all happen."

"T-t-teddy's my friend," stammered Stanley, turning white as a sheet. "I'm g-g-glad I wasn't there. I l-l-live for my p-p-pudding."

"Clam didn't strike me as a bully," said Charlie thoughtfully. "Although, now that I think of it, there did appear to be something untamed about him, despite that snappy haircut of his. As if he had grown up in the Wild or something."

"His c-c-clothes smelled like a c-c-campfire," stammered Stanley. "And I don't think t-t-taking a shower or b-b-bath is p-p-part of his c-c-culture, but I wasn't g-g-going to b-b-bring it up."

And Lila was silent.

Charlie pulled up to the curb. "Here we are," he said. "Back to where we started. Everyone out. I'll see you two bright and early tomorrow morning. Hopefully we'll be seeing Clam again tomorrow too. We'll show him a little PLU—Peace, Love, and Understanding. That'll point him in the right direction, am I right?"

Lila's mom was a paleontologist who spent her days

examining rare and mysterious dinosaur fossils at the Science Academy. She was currently putting together the fossilized remains of a rare bossasaurus skeleton. Her dad was a curator at the Metropolitan Art Gallery. He was currently working on an exhibit of original paintings by Tinto, an African elephant artist that lived at the zoo.

No one knew where Tinto got the idea to make paintings. One day, without any warning, he simply reached out his trunk, seized the big broom that his caretaker used to sweep out his stall, stuck the bristles in a nearby puddle of mud, and began to decorate the wall of his habitat.

The following day, his caretaker brought in some big cans of nontoxic paint and food coloring, and Tinto promptly created a masterpiece. After that, zoo officials chipped in a few elephant-size blank canvases and some brand-new brooms, and Tinto went to town.

Now Lila's dad was arranging Tinto's first art show. It was a challenge getting all those big paintings on the gallery walls and deciding how to hang them right side up, since Tinto was an abstract artist, which made it hard to tell.

The Metropolitan Art Gallery and the Science Academy were both located downtown, and so Lila's parents usually got home later than she did. Every now and then it felt a little rootless and lost to come home to an empty house after a busy day at school, like she was a dandelion seed adrift on a breeze that might go on and on forever without stopping. But today when she opened the door and found an empty house as usual, she was glad more than anything else. Some spot deep inside her was still hot and angry, and the thought of so much empty space helped cool it down.

She decided to take a hot bath to soak out the tension. Her mom usually did that after a difficult day trying to figure out which bone went on what dinosaur and where. "I'm just going to soak out the tension," she'd say and head off to the tub.

So Lila ran the bathwater, went into her mom's bathroom and got some of the special lilac bath crystals that her mom liked to use, and then brought them back to her own bathroom and sprinkled a healthy amount into the hot swirling water.

Then she shucked off her school clothes and got into the tub.

Right away she felt less tense. I should do this more often, she thought.

It's not that she suddenly forgot about Clam's bad behavior. She just didn't take it so personally anymore. In fact, she almost liked him again.

If only Billy Bankson didn't exist! If only he were a fossil fragment, and no one, not even her mom, could figure out how to put his bones back together! She made a few more impossible wishes in a similar vein and then drifted away, thinking about nothing but lilacs.

"Lila," she heard her mom call from downstairs after who knows how much time had gone by. "Lila, are you home?"

Then she heard her up close, right against the bathroom door.

"Lila, are you in there, honey?"

"Yes," Lila answered pleasantly. "I'm in the tub, soaking out the tension."

"Oh, my goodness," said her mom. "That sounds like such a good idea." Then she sounded a little concerned. "Tension?" she asked. "What tension? Is everything all right, honey?"

"Yes," said Lila agreeably. "Everything's fine."

"Don't stay in there too long," said her mom. "You'll wrinkle up like a prune. Dinner will be on the table just as soon as Dad gets home."

Her mom went away, and Lila drifted off again.

"Lila," she heard her dad say after who knows how much more time had passed. He tapped gently on the bathroom door. "Lila, sweetie, dinner's ready. Are you okay in there?"

"Hi, Dad," said Lila contentedly. "I'm fine. How are you?"

"I'm fine too, sweetie," said her dad. "And I'm glad to hear that you're all right. Why don't you come on out now? Dinner's getting cold. And I'm starving. But Mom and I don't want to sit down at the table without you."

"I'm coming," said Lila, and then realized all of a sudden that she really did want to get out of the tub. The water was freezing and she was so wrinkly that she looked like *two* prunes.

Oh, dear, she thought worriedly. Maybe too much of my tension soaked out in the tub!

"Wow, do you ever look like a prune," her mom remarked fondly when she finally sat down at the table. "That must have been a really good soak."

"I'm not going to stay this way, am I? All wrinkly and weird?" Lila asked worriedly.

"Of course not," said her mom. "You know that, honey. Here. Have some mashed potatoes."

"How was your day today, sweetie?" asked her dad.

"Disappointing," said Lila. "There was a new boy in the cab today, and I thought we were going to be friends, but he turned out to be a real jerk."

"We don't use that word, remember?" said her mom. "It's a house rule. But that's too bad, honey. Eat your green beans. What was his name?"

"Clam," said Lila. "Like the mollusk."

There was a sudden stillness at the table. Her parents stopped chewing the food in their mouths and looked down at their plates. To their sensitive ears, Clam sounded an awful lot like Callum, and Callum was the name of Lila's twin brother, the boy they had lost in the woods years ago. Even after all this time, that name was still painful for them to hear.

Uh-oh, thought Lila, sensing the need for ice cream coming on strong.

Fortunately, her parents relaxed again and continued chewing their food.

"It was his first day at school," Lila went on cautiously,

"and everything was going great, but then he made friends with Billy Bankson at lunch and the two of them snuck out of classes for the rest of the day."

"That poor kid," said Lila's dad. "Imagine being new at school and picking Billy Bankson for a friend, of all people. It's about the worst choice you could make."

"I feel sorry for Billy," said her mom understandingly. "He has it tough, with his parents spending so much time without him in the South of France."

"You wouldn't feel sorry for him if you had any pudding at lunch today," said Lila, "because he would have stolen it from you and then forced you to buy it back from him. He made three dollars and fifty cents."

"Billy did that?" asked Lila's dad, and then said to her mom, "Are you sure Hargrove isn't a business school?"

"Don't blame Hargrove," said Lila's mom, who was gifted, bright, and perceptive herself. "I went to school there, remember? And look at how well I turned out. Just like Mary Poppins, I'm practically perfect in every way. I'm just saying that Billy isn't entirely to blame for his bad behavior. If you ask me, his parents should spend less time in the South of France and more time teaching him how to be a useful and productive member of society. Then he might become the kind of guy you really want to make friends with, instead of being such a jerk."

"We don't use that word, remember, dear?" said Lila's dad. "It's a house rule." Lila and her mom laughed.

"I just can't understand why Clam did what he did," said Lila, and both of her parents winced again, despite themselves, at how much it sounded like Callum. "I could tell he liked animals. He barked at a bunch of stray dogs in order to warn them about the dogcatcher."

"In that case, he can't be all bad," said her mom. "You have a way of communicating with animals too."

"Well, I've never tried barking at dogs," said Lila. "But I thought he and I had a special connection. After all, we are the exact same height, and we both have the exact same shade of red hair."

Her parents had stopped chewing again and were staring down at their plates.

Oops, thought Lila. Here comes dessert. I bet it's triple chunk. And then we'll all settle down to watch game shows on TV.

She tried to change the subject. "Guess what?" she said. "My life sciences class is going on a field trip to the zoo. Mr. Sears is taking us. I brought home a permission slip. You have to sign it and include a check for travel expenses."

"Certainly, honey," said her mom, although still in a daze. "That sounds fun. I realize that caging animals is a necessary evil, but I love the zoo."

"I do too," agreed Lila. The city zoo wasn't just cages. There were lots of lovely habitats.

"I should have checked the backseat before we drove away from the campsite that day," her dad said, still in a trance. "It just never occurred to me that a three-year-old boy could undo the restraints on his safety seat. Heck, it was hard enough for *me* to undo those things when I had to, and I had a lot more practice. I should have kept in mind how clever he was."

"No, it was my fault," said Lila's mom somberly. "I strapped him in the seat not twenty minutes before we took off. I obviously didn't do it properly. I was thinking more about dousing the campfire. The only thing I was worried about leaving behind was a single glowing ember, what with it being forest-fire season and all."

"The nerve of that special prosecutor," said Lila's dad, getting angry. "How dare he ever suspect it was foul play?"

"And that awful woman from Social Services who tried to take Lila away," shuddered her mom. "Thank heavens for your sister Donaldina and that sainted Luther. They really saved the day for us."

"Yes, they did," said Lila's dad, "and we'll never lose Lila, as long as we live. But remember, Donaldina told us to put it out of our minds and never think of it again. If we dwell on it, we will go stark raving mad. So the subject is closed, like she said."

He brightened up and served dessert. It was cherry pie, Lila noted with relief.

"Now then," said her dad as he and Lila were rinsing the dinner plates in the kitchen sink later, "I promised you that we would go online tonight and see what we could find out in the way of any breakthroughs or proposals of action that the top scientists in the world might have made to help the polar bears and the penguins. What do you say? Do you still want to do that?"

"Yes," said Lila happily. She loved to go online. They went into her dad's home office, and Lila sat on the fraying rattan stool beside his desk. He fired up his computer and they searched for "polar bear problems" and then "penguin problems" and then "melting ice caps."

"Interesting," said Lila's dad. "Many scientists claim that the polar ice caps are shrinking and will eventually be gone altogether, while others insist that they're only going through a period of decline and will eventually rebound, and still others are saying that there's no change at all, although that sounds a little kooky. But that's the Internet for you. Well, it's not surprising. You can always trust a bunch of scientists not to agree on anything. They think it's much more fun to keep looking for answers than it is to find them." Then he added, "Don't tell your mom I said that. She has a soft spot for scientists, working at the Science Academy as she does."

"I won't tell," Lila promised. She was good at keeping secrets, as long as there was no danger to anyone involved. Danger was *always* a deal-breaker.

"As you know," continued her dad, "the Earth has always gone through weather cycles. All of the deserts in the world were once at the bottom of the sea. Nothing stays the same forever. It's not always a bad thing."

Then they searched for "giant squid" and then "endangered animals" and then "animal doctors" and then "veterinary procedures" and finally "funny animal pictures," and they had a good laugh.

"That's about all the time we have for the computer tonight," said her dad after that. "It's nearly time for bed."

"Can we please look up one more thing?" asked Lila.

"Sure, sweetie," said her dad. "But this has got to be the very last one that we do tonight. What is it?"

" 'Native American names,' " said Lila.

"Any one in particular?" asked her dad.

"Yes," she said. "Firehead."

Her dad looked up "Native American names Firehead." "There's nothing here, sweetie," he said. "The closest thing is 'fire water,' and we don't want to get into that. What made you think of looking up Firehead?"

"That's his name," said Lila. "The boy I met today. Clam Firehead."

"That's certainly an unusual name," said her dad. "Are you sure you heard it right?"

"Yes," said Lila. "And his name wasn't the only unusual thing about him. Charlie the cabbie thought he seemed a little wild. And Stanley Kramer said that he smelled like a campfire. And, like I said before, he and I have the exact same shade of red hair. But don't worry about us being twins or anything like that, Dad. Apart from being the same height and having the same red hair and all, we don't look anything alike."

"But, Lila," said her dad, "your brother and you were fraternal twins, not identical twins. Fraternal twins never look exactly alike. If they did, they'd be identical. If you and your brother were identical twins, you'd both be girls, or you'd both be boys. You know that. We had a talk about it years ago."

"Oh," said Lila. She didn't remember. She must not have been very interested in the subject before. "Well, then. I take it all back."

Her dad was quiet for a minute. He stared at the computer screen like a zombie. Then he switched the computer to sleep mode and said, "Time for bed, sweetie. I'm going to see if there's any ice cream in the freezer. I've got a hankering for some triple chunk."

CHAPTER SIXTEEN

Callum at the Zoo

When the police officer ordered the three Grampas to leave their warm campfire, Callum was determined to help them stand their ground. If he had been Mom or Dad or Aunt Trudy or Uncle Rick or even snaggle-toothed old Grampa, he would have set his ears back, bristled the guard hairs along his shoulders and back, bared his fangs, and then growled and snarled for all he was worth.

But he was only a person, and not a very big one at that.

He *did* have hands instead of paws, however, and he *was* holding a long pointed stick. He was wondering what he should do about that when he heard a distant howl. He couldn't believe his ears! Someone was howling at the full moon, just like he used to do with Mom, Dad, Aunt Trudy, Uncle Rick, and Grampa in the Wild. Then another voice joined in, and then another, and another, until it was a whole chorus of loud, high, wavering cries.

He was instantly overcome with homesickness. His heart swelled nearly to bursting. The distant howling pulled at him like a magnet. The attraction was so strong that he couldn't have resisted it no matter how hard he tried. He reluctantly left Tom, Dick, and Harry to their fate, but was careful to leave them the long pointed stick to do with as they saw fit.

(As it turned out, they left it where it was and went off to the shelter peaceably.)

Callum raced through the park as fast as his feet could carry him, afraid that the howling would stop before he could discover where it was coming from. He found that he was following signs that had ZOO printed on them, and soon discovered a towering iron gate standing in his way, with ZOO spelled in big metal letters on top, and a high brick wall on either side. (Of course, he couldn't read the word. He simply saw its shape.)

The gate and the wall were too steep for him to climb, but he felt such a burning desire to get across that he could hardly keep still. The howling continued, and he even tried jumping, which of course did no good. If only he could get to where the noise was coming from, he thought, then all the bad feelings he'd had since he'd come to the city would be forgotten, and he could carry on the way he had before he'd gotten on the train. He wouldn't feel like a stranger anymore, and he wouldn't feel like such a dummy for spending so much time and effort trying to be a Beta to a half-witted

Alpha like Billy Bankson. And he would no longer feel like such a jerk for betraying Lila and her friends. If he could get to where that howling was coming from, he would be his old self again, through and through!

He hurried along under the high brick wall, following the sound, and soon came to a place where it seemed to come directly from the other side. A thick elm tree was growing by the wall there, which had branches low enough that he could reach them. He lifted himself up and slowly and carefully made his way to the outermost limbs until he was suspended high above the ground on the other side of the wall.

At first glance, there didn't seem to be much difference between the zoo on this side of the wall and the park on the side that he had come from. There was a similar rolling expanse of green lawn and the same kinds of leafy trees and thick banks of bushes. But when he looked more carefully, he spotted some important differences.

Off on the far side of the lawn, for example, what looked like an empty concrete canyon stretched along the green, and running along the far side of that was a long fence with pointy metal bars. And it looked like part of a mountaintop had fallen off and landed in the center of the lawn. The rocky chunk reminded him of his craggy home in the Wild, except a lot easier to climb.

Looking down at the ground directly beneath him, he quickly identified an Alpha Male, a Beta Male, a Beta

Female, and an Omega in a family of North American Gray Wolves or Timber Wolves (*Canis lupus*) gathered on the grass. And they were the ones that were doing the howling.

Hearing it from up close, he could tell it was an unmotivated effort, like they were only howling out of habit, not for fun. And it seemed that they spent a lot of time gabbing in between. At least they did in his homesick imagination. You could say that, under the circumstances, his imagination ran Wild.

"I don't know why we're always gathering here by the wall," complained the Beta Male in the same cranky growl as Uncle Rick's. "We've got all this space in our habitat, and yet we're still always here by the wall."

"I like to know just where my freedom ends," snarled the Alpha Male, sounding exactly like Dad.

"Always playing the tough guy," barked the Omega, who, like Grampa, was a crusty old coot. "Don't forget, tough guy, you were born into a show-business family, same as the rest of us."

"I do so love the stage," whimpered the Beta Female. "Every time I growl and snarl and scare some poor audience member half to death, I get a chill."

"Zip it," snarled the Alpha Male. "Time for another howl."

The group commenced howling again, but it didn't come anywhere near the expression of sheer joy and abandon that Callum remembered so dearly. It's as if they can't be bothered to do it right, he thought, wondering why. If Mom and

Dad and Aunt Trudy and Uncle Rick and Grampa saw a full moon like the one that was out tonight, they'd be howling their lungs out.

"I'm just not in the mood to howl tonight," whimpered the Beta Female. "It's not the same without the whole pack here. I wish Mary would come out of the nocturnal enclosure and join us."

"I'm worried about her too," growled the Beta Male. "She hasn't left the nocturnal enclosure for three days now."

"She's all right," snarled the Alpha Male. "She's just stubborn, is all."

"Stubborn?" barked the Omega. "It's her wounded pride, more like it. She's sulking. I never saw an Alpha Female so stuck-up. And I've been in show business all my life."

"It's not her fault her feelings were hurt," whimpered the Beta Female. "And besides, she's still recuperating."

"Recuperating?" barked the Omega. "All that was wrong with her was a measly dewclaw infection. She only spent a single night in the veterinary hospital. And that's where her pride was hurt, and now it's causing her more pain than her infected dewclaw ever did."

"Watch what you say about my wife," snarled the Alpha Male.

"Oh, go soak your head, you big lug," the Omega barked rudely.

Wow, thought Callum. Grampa talked back to Dad, all right, but he would never have dared to say anything as bold as that. Clearly, this city pack was operating by a whole other set of rules than those in the Wild.

"For what it's worth," whimpered the Beta Female, "I'm on Mary's side. Why should that snow leopard have gotten special treatment in the veterinary hospital? They were both in there together."

"Because that snow leopard was about a hundred and sixty years old," barked the Omega. "And her poor creaky joints were swollen and sore. She needed that carpet to lay on."

"Well," whimpered the Beta Female, "they should have given Mary a carpet to lay on too."

"Mary didn't need a carpet," barked the Omega. "She's barely two years old. There's nothing wrong with her joints!"

"That's not the point," whimpered the Beta Female. "It's a question of fairness. My feelings would be hurt too, if it had happened to me."

"Feelings, schmeelings," barked the Omega. "Don't be such a crybaby."

"Shut your traps, all of you," snarled the Alpha Male. "It's time to howl again."

Once more the pack commenced howling, and once more it was a halfhearted effort. I simply can't stand this for another minute, thought Callum. If he didn't howl soon, he was going to bust a gut. He opened his mouth and let loose a howl that contained all of his frustration and rage, and all of his longing for home, and all of the love that he had for all the good things that the Great Spirit provided. And when he was done, he was clean out of breath.

Everyone in the pack was duly impressed. "Finally," snarled the Alpha Male to the others, "you got your act together. That sounded pretty decent, for a change."

"I haven't howled like that in years," barked the Omega. "Too bad there wasn't an audience to hear it."

"I've got chills," whimpered the Beta Female.

"I bet even Mary heard that, in the nocturnal enclosure," growled the Beta Male.

"Let's do it again," snarled the Alpha Male, "now that we've got it right."

And they were just about to open their mouths again when Callum fell out of the tree.

He had been so engrossed in howling that he had forgotten to hold on tight to the branch, and when he finally got his breath back, he lost his grip altogether and came down with a crash.

To say that the pack was startled to see him fall out of the sky and land in their midst would be the understatement of the year. The Alpha Male, the Beta Male, the Beta Female, and the Omega were all shocked out of their wits. They put their tails between their legs and ran for their lives.

The fall, or rather the landing, knocked the wind out of Callum, but in a moment he got up and brushed himself off. And that's when the Alpha Male came to his senses.

"Stop running for your lives and take your tails out from

between your legs," he snarled at the rest of the pack. "Follow me in attack formation, and make it snappy!"

"Oh, goody," growled the Beta Male. "We haven't attacked anything in years. Or ever, as a matter of fact."

"I don't know about you," snarled the Alpha Male, "but I've been saving it up for a moment like this."

"I've got chills," whimpered the Beta Female again. It was clearly her favorite thing to say.

"Too bad we don't have an audience," barked the Omega. "This will be our best show of the season!"

They set back their ears, bristled the guard hairs along their shoulders and backs, raised their muzzles, narrowed their eyes, bared their fangs, and growled and snarled for all they were worth. That's just what Mom and Dad and Aunt Trudy and Uncle Rick and Grampa would have done, Callum thought approvingly.

He knew what he had to do too.

He rolled over onto his back, exposing his vulnerable throat and underside.

The whole pack quit stalking him and gaped in astonishment.

"Bless my tail and whiskers!" barked the Omega. "It's an audience member! What's it doing on this side of the fence?"

"And more importantly," growled the Beta Male, "why is it rolling on its back like that?"

"It looks like it's trying to be a turtle," whimpered the Beta Female.

"Why in the world does it want to be a turtle?" growled the Beta Male.

"I'm not trying to be a turtle," said Callum. "I'm demonstrating submissive behavior to show you that I'm not a danger or a threat to the pack."

But of course, since he had spoken to them in his own language, all the pack heard was a weird kind of groan and something that sounded like a hiccup. Zoo animals or not, they were still wolves.

Uh-oh, he thought worriedly. Big mistake. What was I thinking? I ought to talk to them like Dad used to do instead.

"Woof! Woof!" he said fervently, trying his best to get the meaning of submissive behavior across in the language of the Wild. "Yip, yip, yip! Grrr!"

"Why in heaven's name is it making those awful sounds?" whimpered the Beta Female. "It's hurting my ears!"

"What does it mean by submental behavior?" growled the Beta Male. "Is it making fun of us?"

"So what if it *is* an audience member," snarled the Alpha Male. "I say we kill it and eat it anyway. I've got a hankering for fresh blood!"

"You're giving me chills," whimpered the Beta Female, who must have been absolutely frozen by now. Then she added excitedly, "Hold on. Let me tell Mary about this. If this doesn't get her to leave the nocturnal enclosure, then I don't know what will!"

Callum didn't move a muscle. He was thoroughly

disappointed to be reminded of how poorly he spoke wolf language when he was around the real thing. The rest of the pack stood guard over him, drooling like crazy, their red tongues licking their razor-sharp teeth as they anticipated ripping him to bloody shreds.

The Alpha Male stood so close that Callum could smell his hot breath. It smelled like raw meat.

The Beta Female returned from the nocturnal enclosure alone. "Mary's worse off than I thought," she whimpered sadly. "She said, 'So what?' and doesn't want to join the kill. She did ask that we save her the pancreas, however, if nobody else wants it."

"If she wants the pancreas, she can come get it herself," barked the Omega.

"Watch your tone," snarled the Alpha Male, then said, "that's my wife you're talking about."

"Yeah, yeah, tough guy," barked the Omega. "Keep your tail on. She can have the pancreas. What do I care? I want the heart. I want to rip it out and take a bite out of it while it's still beating!"

Callum didn't look forward to that.

"Does everyone remember how to kill live prey?" snarled the Alpha Male. "Or do we have to go over it again?"

Callum tried to look extra submissive. Why wasn't it working? he wondered. It was crazy that this pack didn't know the meaning of rolling onto your back and exposing your vulnerable throat and underside! What kind of wolves were they, anyhow?

"All right, then," snarled the Alpha Male. "We attack on the count of three. Teeth bared? Claws out? One, two . . ."

Callum shut his eyes and prepared for the worst.

Just then, the beam of a powerful flashlight cut across the lawn.

"*Hold it right there!*" came a sudden sharp voice, speaking in Callum's own language.

The pack yelped in alarm and raced away toward the trees with their tails between their legs again.

Callum squinted as the flashlight's beam hit him full in the face.

"Who are you?" demanded the voice in a tone so loud and piercing that it could probably have been heard halfway across the globe. "And how did you get here?"

"My name is Clam Firehead," said Callum. "Like the mollusk. And I fell out of that tree."

"I was attacked by a giant clam off the coast of Bermuda," said the voice, sounding calmer now, but still gravely serious. The flashlight's beam moved away, and Callum could make out the profile of a short, stocky man standing over him.

"The belligerent marine bivalve nearly bit my legs off," the stranger went on. "When I finally wrestled that baby onto the boat, it was clam chowder for my island guides for a week. But it's no time to go jogging down memory lane. Do you realize how close you came to being devoured alive? Those animals with the razor-sharp teeth and deadly claws are North American Gray Wolves or Timber Wolves, *Canis lupus*. And they're as mean and deadly as mean and deadly ever gets. They'll tear off your head as soon as look at you!"

"They were planning to rip out my heart and take a bite out of it while it was still beating," said Callum.

"Oh they were, were they?" the stranger said grimly. "I wouldn't put it past them, the brutes."

"Thank you for saving me," said Callum, then asked, "Who are *you*, if you don't mind my asking?"

With the flick of his wrist, the stranger lit up his own face with the flashlight's powerful beam.

It was a terrible sight. There wasn't anything special about the rest of the man's face, but there was something horribly wrong with his nose.

"Yes, it's true," he said importantly. "Your eyes do not deceive you. I'm Buzz Optigon, the world-famous wildlife wrangler, at your service. Now, we'd better get out of this here habitat before those wolves come back, or we're in deep doo-doo, and I'm not just whistling 'Dixie'!"

CHAPTER SEVENTEEN

Callum and Buzz

You look chilled to the bone," said world-famous wildlife wrangler Buzz Optigon, shining his flashlight directly into Callum's face again. "And your eyes look all squinty and strange. Oh, that's just because of the flashlight! Sorry. Come with me. I'll make you a nice cup of soup. We'll decide where to take things from there. My brain always works better when I've got some nourishing food in my belly, and I'll bet yours is no different."

He directed the flashlight's powerful beam ahead of them to lead the way.

At the end of the lawn, they came to the concrete canyon that Callum had spotted from his perch in the treetop. Buzz took out a key and unlocked a thick metal screen door that led to a walkway across to the other side, where he unlocked a second metal screen door and then locked it behind them again.

Now they were on the other side of the pointy metal bars, and Callum could see that the pack had gotten over their fright and returned. They didn't look very happy. The Alpha Male, the Beta Male, the Beta Female, and the Omega were snarling at him angrily and gnashing their teeth. But they couldn't come anywhere near him now that he was safely behind the fence.

Buzz led him down a long concrete walkway. They passed concession stands and information booths, all closed, of course, since it was the middle of the night, and they passed other fences as well, behind which who knows what dangerous animals were lurking. Perhaps the snow leopard from the veterinary hospital is behind one of those fences, thought Callum curiously. But then he had only imagined hearing about that, hadn't he?

"You're lucky I came by when I did," said Buzz. "You can thank the full moon for that. After all of my years in the Wild, I'm pretty darn sensitive to the lunar pull. I was taking a little stroll in the moonlight, working on my moon-tan, when all of a sudden I heard something that I haven't heard in years: a full-throated demonstration of North American Gray Wolf lung power. Nothing like it has ever come out of the mollycoddled specimens we've got around here before, no matter how tough that Alpha Male pretends to be. I didn't know what in tarnation had gotten into those lily-livered beasts. And then I caught sight of you in the beam of my high-powered flashlight, and I knew what the explanation was. It was the presence of live prey that had gotten them so riled up."

By that time, they had reached a little cabin across from the public toilets. It was so small, and it blended so well into its surroundings, that you could have walked right past it without even knowing it was there.

"The zoo officials are letting me stay here while I write my memoirs," said Buzz. "They want to publish all the stories I've got after forty-odd years of wildlife wrangling, and I plan to give them every last one. I figure it'll take me at least five years to write them all down. Six, if I take the time to spell all of the words correctly."

He unlocked the door and led Callum inside. It was a small cabin, and everything inside it was small. There was a small wooden table and two small wooden chairs beside a small sink and a small kitchen range, and a small bed in the corner, neatly made. Every inch of the four small walls was covered with photographs of wild animals, all taken at close range. Most of the photos appeared to have been taken just as the wild animal was attacking the photographer.

"I took all of those shots myself," Buzz said proudly. "I only lost ten or twelve cameras in the process. Three of them were actually eaten. I don't think they were swallowed, or at least I hope not, because that's not good for anyone's digestion, not even a Tasmanian thunder goat's. But they were chewed up, all right, into itty-bitty pieces."

He motioned toward the small wooden table. "Sit

yourself down," he said. "The first thing we're going to do is get some hot soup inside you. Then we'll call up your mom and dad and go from there."

Callum knew that wouldn't do any good. The only mom and dad he knew didn't have a phone, and even if they did, they wouldn't have been able to work it with their paws. He himself had only just learned about phones because Billy Bankson and James each had one. But he didn't say anything about that.

Buzz puttered around the small kitchen and then brought a steaming bowl of soup to the table. "Wait till it cools," he said, placing it in front of Callum. "Then drink it straight from the bowl. It's miso, and it will do you a world of good. I first heard about miso soup when I was in Japan trying to infiltrate a herd of wild boar. The nurse at the hospital who bandaged my tusk punctures served it to me twice a day, and I recovered in half the time the surgeon expected me to."

Callum blew on the hot soup till it cooled, then lifted the bowl to his mouth and took a sip. Sure enough, it was delicious, if a little salty. Right away it made him feel stronger and more alive.

"Now, about your mom and dad," said Buzz, picking up the phone. "Where can we reach them?"

"They're up in the woods," Callum answered truthfully. "And they don't have a phone."

"Sounds like me, back in the day," Buzz said nostalgically.

"I pretty much shunned all forms of technology except for my Nintendo and my portable fax machine. They didn't take you with them?"

"They took me to the train station," replied Callum.

"They sent you home, eh?" said Buzz. "Why? What did you do? You can tell me. Just between you and me and the mailbox, I've gotten into plenty of trouble in my time. Oh. Right. Judging by your blazer, you probably had to get back to school. Well, where do you live then? What's your address?"

Callum was silent. Here, he thought after a while. This is my address.

"You're awfully quiet," said Buzz, sounding serious. "I bet I know what you're thinking, and I'll tell you straight off. This isn't the nose I was born with. A year ago last Saturday I was in the Ozark Mountains photographing the mating display of a pair of striped chipmunks when I was unexpectedly ambushed by a rogue porcupine. Before I could defend myself properly, the enraged rodent bit my schnozzle clean off. The doctor in the emergency room at the hospital made me a new one using parts of my stomach and upper thigh. I think it looks pretty good, all things considered, but it's a sight that takes a little getting used to. I don't blame the porcupine, although I'd like to know what had made it so angry. All I can think of is that it just didn't like my designer cologne. The thing I regret most is that I'll never smell the delicious aroma of fried liver and runny cheese again."

Callum was properly horrified to hear about the rogue porcupine and what it had done to Buzz's schnozzle. But it didn't surprise him. He had never met a porcupine that wasn't all worked up about one thing or another, and he had always steered as far away from them as possible.

"We can call up your school in the morning," said Buzz. "Dawn will be here in a couple of hours anyway. But tell me, how did you happen to be up in that tree by the wolf habitat in the first place?"

"I was answering the call of the Wild," Callum said honestly, and Buzz nodded understandingly.

"You're a man after my own heart," he said. "You should try taking a camera next time. But I'll tell you, you're darn lucky the whole pack wasn't out there tonight. The Alpha Female is a coldhearted piece of work. She would have buried her snout in your belly and ripped out your insides without so much as a how-do-you-do. Something's up with her lately. She hasn't left the nocturnal enclosure for days. It's a doggone shame. The zoo just spent half a million dollars upgrading the wolf habitat, and she's not even enjoying it."

"I'm sorry to hear that," said Callum, as if he hadn't heard all about it already from the rest of the pack. Which was true. He had only imagined it. "It sounds like she's not feeling well."

"Oh, she had a minor infection on her dewclaw," said Buzz. "The zoo officials put her in the veterinary hospital for a night, just to be sure it wasn't serious. It's all cleared up now."

Callum couldn't believe his ears. A dewclaw infection? That was what the wolves had said, in his imagination!

"Was she all alone at the hospital?" he asked a little nervously.

"No, there was an ancient old snow leopard in there that was suffering from multiple aches and pains, poor thing," said Buzz. "They had to set down a carpet for her to lie on to rest her weary bones."

"And they didn't lay down the same kind of carpet for the Alpha Female?" asked Callum. Had he actually heard what those wolves had been saying? No, it wasn't possible. It had to be a coincidence. But what a coincidence!

"No, they didn't set down a carpet for the Alpha Female," said Buzz. "They didn't think she needed one." Then his eyes lit up as he put two and two together. "You think the Alpha Female was jealous of that snow leopard for getting to lie on the carpet?" he asked. "I wouldn't put it past her. She's got the biggest ego of any animal I've ever seen."

"Maybe you should put down a piece of carpet on the lawn for her now," said Callum, "and see if she comes out of the nocturnal enclosure to claim it."

"That's a darn good idea," said Buzz. "It's worth a try, anyway. Say," he said to Callum admiringly, "you're a regular wolf whisperer, you are. Do you have the same insight into other animals' lives, or just wolves?"

"Just wolves, I guess," said Callum, "and stray dogs," which was true too. Forget about human beings. They confused the heck out of him.

"Now then," said Buzz, clearing away the empty soup bowl, "since there's no way to get you back to where you belong until morning, I suggest you get a little shut-eye. You can sleep on that bed over there, on top of the covers. I'll throw a nice quilt over you."

He went to the cupboard and brought out a warm, fluffy quilt with a colorful pattern of squares and triangles on it.

"A kindly old nurse in New Mexico gave this to me when I was in the hospital after being attacked by a blood-sucking chupacabra," he said. "Some people will tell you that chupacabras don't exist. I happen to know otherwise. I learned it the hard way, and I had exactly two hundred and fifty stitches to prove it. I would have had photographic evidence too, if my camera hadn't disappeared down a bottomless gully. I was forced to drop it, you see. I needed both hands to protect my face. I'd just gotten my new schnozzle installed, and I knew that devilish chupacabra would try to rip it off first thing."

Callum would have said something sympathetic, but as soon as he lay down on the small, neat bed he was out like a light.

He woke up a few hours later to the sound of rain beating on the cabin roof. He opened his eyes. The room was empty, and it was light outside. The rain beat steadily. He felt so warm and comfortable on Buzz Optigon's small, neat bed that he wanted to stay there forever. That was one thing he could say in favor of his newfound species. They certainly knew how to make a comfy den when they wanted to.

He thought back to the events of the night before. Was it possible that he actually understood wolf language? He hoped so. The thought that Mom had actually called him Little Pig Face and Salty Lollipop in a loving manner made him feel warm and fuzzy inside. It was a good feeling, the best he'd had in a long, long time.

The rain came down harder, and he dropped off to sleep again.

When he woke up once more, sunlight was pouring through the windows. Birds were chirping, and he heard a few other sounds that made him sit up with a start. An elephant trumpeted, for one, and a peacock mewed, for another, and although he knew they were all animal sounds, they may as well have come from another planet as far as he was concerned. As usual, the thought of the unknown made him kind of nervous, but then he quickly got excited, in a happy way.

How could he have forgotten? He was at the zoo!

He jumped out of bed, neatly folded the warm, fluffy quilt from New Mexico, and ran over to look out the kitchen window.

There was a handwritten note on the small table. It said:

GOOD MORNING, CLAM FIREHEAD, IF THAT IS
YOUR REAL NAME. HERE IS A BANANA THAT I
TOOK FROM THE MONKEYS' BREAKFAST CART.
I DON'T THINK THEY WILL MISS IT. THEY GET
ENOUGH FRESH FRUIT IN THE MORNING TO
FEED A WHOLE COUNTRY. EAT IT IF YOU ARE
HUNGRY. THEN WASH YOUR FACE AND HANDS
IN THE SINK AND MEET ME BY THE SPOT
WHERE I FOUND YOU LAST NIGHT, ONLY ON
THE OTHER SIDE OF THE FENCE. OKAY? OKAY.
YOUR FRIEND, BUZZ OPTIGON, THE WORLD-
FAMOUS WILDLIFE WRANGLER.

Naturally, Callum couldn't read a single word of it, but
Buzz had included a helpful diagram with plenty of pictures of monkeys and a banana and an arrow pointing to a
map that showed where the wolf habitat was located, which
made the note easy to read for someone who had never
read a note before. He had even included a smiley face by
his name.

Callum devoured the banana after thanking the Great
Spirit, washed his face and hands in the sink, used the bathroom, washed his hands again, and then raced outside, shut-
ting the cabin door behind him.

At first he didn't recognize the place. Unlike last night,
when the zoo was closed, there were a lot of people milling
around now. They all seemed to be headed in the same
direction.

"What's going on? Where's everyone going?" he heard one of the passersby ask another.

"Tinto the genius painter elephant is painting another masterpiece today!" the other passerby answered excitedly.

"Did you hear that, kids?" the first passerby said to the two fussy toddlers he was pushing in a bright blue stroller. "Tinto the genius painter elephant is painting another masterpiece. Let's go watch!"

And he quickly turned the bright blue stroller around to follow after all the other Tinto fans.

"That boring genius painter elephant is painting another boring masterpiece," another passerby said to his friend. "Which means that the rest of the zoo will be practically empty until he runs out of inspiration. Let's go see the lemurs!"

Callum tried to recall how he had gotten to the cabin the night before, and then set off in what his instinct told him was the proper direction. His instinct was correct, and he soon spotted Buzz up ahead. Buzz was busy polishing a large painted sign.

"Hola, Clam," said the world-famous wildlife wrangler with a smile that rose up at both sides of his mangled schnozzle. "Just giving this sign a little spit polish. I'm sure the zoo would like people to see what it says."

"What does it say?" asked Callum interestedly.

"'North American Gray Wolf or Timber Wolf, *Canis lupus*,' of course," said Buzz. "Do you remember what we talked about last night? Looky over there."

Callum peered over the fence at the timber wolf habitat and saw a big Alpha Female sitting on a patch of plush carpet on the lawn, grinning from ear to ear. Wow, he thought. She sure loves that carpet!

"I wouldn't have believed it if I hadn't seen it with my own two eyes," said Buzz. "Your hunch was right. It was that carpet she wanted all along. Next thing you know, she'll want a couch and a big fancy chair to go with it. Funny thing is, it rained like crazy just an hour ago. That darn carpet is soaking wet. But look at her. She won't budge."

The Alpha Female continued to grin like she'd just won the lottery. The rest of the pack gathered around her.

"Hi, Mary," Callum imagined he heard the Beta Female say to her, whimpering earnestly. "Don't you want to get up off that soaking wet carpet? Even the wet grass is drier than that. Seeing you sitting on that cold wet thing is giving me chills. Real chills, I mean."

"Don't come any closer, Beth Ann," snapped the Alpha Female. "This carpet is mine. Mine! Do you hear?"

"Great," barked the Omega, rolling his eyes. "First she wouldn't leave the nocturnal enclosure. Now she won't get up off that soggy carpet."

"What do you expect?" growled the Beta Male. "She's as stubborn as ten mules put together."

"Watch what you say," snarled the Alpha Male. "That's my wife you're talking about. And what I want to know is, who told that darn wildlife wrangler that Mary wanted to lie on a carpet in the first place?"

The whole pack stared at Callum. He tried to look like he wasn't paying any attention to them, although he couldn't stop trying to imagine what they were saying. It was a hard habit to break.

"You think it was the prey?" he heard the Omega bark in disbelief.

"We should have clawed it to pieces when we had the chance," growled the Beta Male. "Now it's too late. If only we hadn't hesitated."

"No hesitating next time," snarled the Alpha Male, baring his fangs.

"Seems like they still want a taste of your hide," said Buzz to Callum. "Believe me, I've seen that look enough times to know."

At that moment, a zoo official came by, talking into a walkie-talkie. She noticed Buzz and Callum. "Forget it, I just found him," she said, signing off. "I'll talk to you later. Save me some popcorn."

She went up to Callum and Buzz with a frown on her face. "There you are," she said accusingly. Callum flinched. Somehow, he was expecting to get into trouble again. But the zoo official turned to Buzz instead. "I've been instructed to remind you that under no circumstances are you to introduce foreign objects into any of the animal habitats, Mr. Optigon," she informed him sternly. "Do it again, and the zoo will be forced to take away your access keys. You've got permission to observe the animals only, not to interact with them."

Then she spotted the Alpha Female sitting on the carpet.

"Holy cow!" she said. "What do you know? The Alpha Female actually came out of the nocturnal enclosure!"

"She just needed a little incentive," said Buzz, looking at Callum proudly.

"Well, we've still got to get that carpet out of there," said the zoo official.

"You try taking it away from her," said Buzz. "We'll notify your next of kin."

"Maybe we can dye the carpet green," said the zoo official, looking nervously at the Alpha Female's razor-sharp teeth and deadly claws, "to match the grass."

Then she took a good look at Callum, noting his blazer in particular. "Say, you're here early," she said. "How did you get off the bus before the others?"

What bus? thought Callum. What others?

Then he looked out over the bluff, where a stretch of the zoo's parking lot could be seen. A big yellow bus was just squeezing into a parking space. The doors opened, and students from the Hargrove School for the Gifted, Bright, and Perceptive Child began to pile out.

One of the first off the bus, Callum noticed, was Lila.

CHAPTER EIGHTEEN
Lila at the Zoo

Mr. Sears ought to be commended for assigning your class that report," Lila's dad had said at the breakfast table bright and early that morning. "Some of our fellow creatures on this planet are definitely getting the short end of the stick. Figuring out a way to help them isn't going to be easy. The more ideas there are to work with, the better. I think that what you and your Hargrove friends have come up with is a pretty good start."

"I can't tell you how glad I am to hear that," said her mom. "I've been worrying every day about those poor unfortunate animals. Another slice of banana for you, Lila?"

"We can't stop worrying about them completely," said Lila. "They aren't out of the woods yet. In all probability they're going to face a lot of difficult challenges down the road. But that's to be expected for everyone. In order to survive, you've got to be able to adapt to all sorts of circumstances. Yes, please, I'll have some more banana. Thanks, Mom."

"It sounds like you've given the subject a good deal of thought," said her mom.

"I have," said Lila. "And I've learned from experience. Remember when we lost what's-his-name in the woods? We adapted to life after that because we had no choice but to get on with our lives. And one day we might even go camping again."

Even though Lila had been careful to say "what's-his-name" instead of "Callum," both her parents cringed.

"You've been a brave little girl, sweetie," said Lila's dad to Lila, trying to be strong. "And you're right, we've moved on. Although it looks like we will never again gather around the kitchen table with your fraternal, not identical, twin brother, who would be exactly your height, with the same exact shade of bright red hair as yours, he will live forever in our hearts."

"Amen to that," said Lila's mom, with tears in her eyes.

"And now what's on our agendas for today?" asked her dad, bravely getting on with life as usual.

"I'm going on the field trip to the zoo," said Lila. "Which reminds me. Where's my signed permission slip and check for travel expenses? Where, where, where?"

"Here you go, honey," said her mom, handing it over. "Don't have a cow."

"What are you doing today, dear?" Lila's dad asked her mom.

"I'm going to try to figure out what to do with that darn bossasaurus bone that I dusted off yesterday," said Lila's mom. "I had it earmarked as an arm bone at first, but I thought it over in bed last night and now I'm pretty sure that it's a leg bone instead. So I'm going to switch it and see if it fits."

"The head bone's connected to the leg bone," Lila's dad started singing. "The neck bone's connected to the . . ."

"*Shoulder bone!*" yelled Lila, and everyone laughed.

"There's no yelling at the table, remember? It's a house rule," said Lila's mom, pretending to disapprove, although she was laughing too.

"Sorry," said Lila with a grin.

"As for myself, I'm headed down to the zoo as well this morning," her dad said after that. "Tinto the genius painter elephant is giving every indication that he's about to create another masterpiece."

"Don't get too close to that genius painter elephant while he's painting, dear," said Lila's mom. "You're wearing your second-best tie. You don't want to be part of a Tinto master-piece yourself."

"Don't worry," said her dad. "I'll keep my distance. Let's be off, then. We'll rendezvous again here tonight around six and touch base at dinner."

Stanley was waiting at the corner as usual, but Lila noticed disappointedly that there was no sign of Clam Fire-head.

"You're so l-l-lucky," stammered Stanley, who knew all about what the students in the Yellow Level were up to that day. "I l-l-love the zoo. I don't think it's an animal p-p-prison. I'd like to have my own h-h-habitat."

"It's a necessary evil," said Lila wisely. "Many zoo animals were born at the zoo and would be unable to compete in the Wild. The zoo is their natural home."

"That's t-t-true," stammered Stanley.

"So, our mysterious friend is still playing hooky, eh?" said Charlie the cabbie after Lila and Stanley got in the back of the cab. "Too bad that darn Billy Bankson is such a powerful influence. I wish his parents would wake up and smell the coffee already. Am I right?"

"We've all got to adapt in order to survive," said Lila smartly. "It's understandable that we should make a few mistakes along the way."

"Truer words were never spoken," said Charlie. "You're a real humanitarian, Lila, full of PLU—Peace, Love, and Understanding."

"I think so t-t-too," stammered Stanley devotedly, although he didn't really know that "humanitarian" meant a caring, kind, and compassionate person.

"Thank you," said Lila. "I'm trying extra hard lately."

There was still no Clam in Mr. Sears's life sciences class. But Billy was there, stealing other people's homework assignments to call his own before the bell rang. Jose Alvarez and John Mason joined in, stealing other people's homework assignments too. Roger Phipps, however, took no part in it.

"Give it back," Roger told them sternly.

"Who died and made you king?" complained Jose and John, but they returned the homework they'd stolen anyway. They always obeyed Roger. He wasn't bigger than they were, but he had a way of speaking that made them want to do what he said, pronto.

Tito Jones and Curtis Takahashi looked at Roger as if he were their hero. But Billy never listened to anyone, not even Roger, and so he kept the homework he'd stolen.

"You're despicable," Becca Adams told him, standing her ground. "You can have my homework only when you pry it from my cold dead fingers."

"Ha-ha!" laughed Billy. "You can keep it in your cold dead fingers. I don't need your homework. I've got plenty already."

"It's not fair," said Rachel Cohen. "I slaved all night on that paper."

"Don't worry," Becca assured her. "Even if Billy erases your name and writes his own on your paper instead, it won't fool Mr. Sears. Mr. Sears knows all of our handwriting like he knows the back of his hand. He'll still give you credit."

Lila walked up to Billy's desk and got right in his face. "Where is he?" she demanded. "What did you do to him?"

"What did I do to who?" replied Billy, ignorant of the fact that he should have said "to whom."

"You know who!" said Lila. "Clam Firehead!"

"What did I do to *him*?" Billy exclaimed defensively. "You mean what did he do to *me*! I'll tell you what! First he got me into trouble with the police in the park, and then he made a mess in my bedroom after I was nice enough to invite him home for a sleepover. Frieda, my housekeeper, baked a three-cheese lasagna especially for us, and he acted like he didn't even notice, which really hurt her feelings. And after all that, he walked out in the middle of the night without even saying good-bye or thank you or anything."

"I don't believe you," said Lila. "And if it is true that he took so much advantage of you, it only goes to show that you can't stand up for yourself without your goons around to protect you."

By "goons" she meant Jose, John, and Roger. Jose and John looked pleased and proud of it, like they had just won a prize or something. Roger, though, looked upset. His face turned a rosy red under its usual brown, and he stared at the floor.

"All right, class," said Mr. Sears, coming into the room. "I know you're completely ecstatic to be going on a field trip, but try to contain yourselves. We'll be lining up for the bus to the zoo in twenty minutes. But first, I'll be collecting your homework. Everyone, please pass your papers forward."

The class passed their papers forward, and Mr. Sears collected the bunch.

"Hmmm," he said, leafing through the pile. "Rachel, it appears that you've written Billy's name on your paper by mistake. Let me change it back for you."

"Okay," said Rachel, grinning.

"Aw, shoot," said Billy.

"Are you still worried about that new kid?" Becca asked Lila on the bus to the zoo. They were sitting together in one of the few seats that wasn't all tattered and torn. The bus was at least seventy years old. Rachel and Curtis were sitting in the row across the aisle. Poor Tito had to fend for himself somewhere in the back. Everyone was trying not to breathe too deeply because the air was full of engine exhaust.

"Clam will be all right," said Becca. "You said so yourself. You've got to adapt if you want to survive, right?"

"But that's why I'm worried," said Lila. "He's trying to adapt, but I don't think he can do it fast enough to survive. You saw how different he is. He acts like he's never seen a city before, like he's never been to school, like he's never even tasted enough food to know that sloppy joes are disgusting. Everything seems new to him. It's like he came from another world, as if he grew up in the Wild or something and was raised by wolves . . ."

Lila was suddenly quiet. Some powerful new idea had driven everything else from her mind. She looked out the window at the passing scenery and thoughtfully tugged at a lock of her bright red hair.

Clam's bright red hair . . . C-l-a-m . . .

"I admit he's different and all," said Becca. "But I don't think he's *that* different. I mean, get real! No one is raised by wolves these days."

With a loud rumbling sound from its engine and a terrible squealing of its brakes, the Hargrove bus lurched into the zoo parking lot.

"Quiet down, people. I want everyone to exit the bus in single file," said Mr. Sears.

Lila passed Billy on her way out the door. Billy was hanging back, hiding in one of the empty seat rows so that he could jump out and frighten some poor victim out of his lunch money. It was probably going to be Tito. Tito knew it and was staying put in his seat at the back.

"If it turns out that Clam is *lost* or *hurt*," Lila told Billy, spitting the words in his face, she was so angry, "then I'm going to *sue* you for *every cent you've got*. My uncle Luther is a successful lawyer, as well as a former heavyweight boxing champion. He's *never* lost a case."

"So what?" scoffed Billy. "I'm not afraid of you. My dad's got lawyers too."

"*Bring 'em on*," said Lila fiercely.

Billy's eyes got big and he slipped past her and ran off the bus.

"It's okay, Tito," Lila called to the back. "You can come out now. The coast is clear."

"Gather around," Mr. Sears told the class when everyone,

including Tito Jones, was safely off the bus. "I've got a treat in store for you. Tinto the genius painter elephant is creating another one of his monumental masterpieces today. I'm sure none of you wants to miss the opportunity to see Tinto do his thing. So let's proceed to the elephant habitat in an orderly fashion."

There was a huge crowd at the main viewing area of the elephant habitat, but space had been reserved for students on field trips, and the Hargrove contingent excitedly moved toward the front.

Tinto the genius painter elephant was indeed painting a masterpiece, if you call slapping a broom soaked in paint against a big blank canvas "painting a masterpiece." He appeared to be enjoying himself as much as the crowd was enjoying watching him. After every slap of the broom, he flapped his enormous ears and bobbed his gigantic head up and down as if he were laughing like crazy, and the crowd cheered and applauded.

Three other elephants stood nearby, and after every slap of his brush they raised their trunks and trumpeted and flapped their ears as if they were getting a good laugh out of it too.

Some genius elephant, thought Lila. He's just showing off!

"Isn't it amazing?" Mr. Sears said to the class. "Obviously human beings aren't the only mammals who can express themselves through art."

Tinto continued slapping the broom against the canvas and laughing, and the crowd continued cheering and applauding. Honestly, thought Lila. Zoos are a necessary evil, but do we really need this charade?

Rrrriiiipppp!

Oops! Tinto had swung the paint-laden broom a little too hard. It had torn right through the canvas material.

A groan went up from the crowd.

Tinto looked embarrassed. His ears wilted, and his trunk drooped to the ground, but the other elephants trumpeted and flapped their ears as if they were laughing their heads off.

"Don't worry, folks," announced a zoo official. "It'll just take us twenty or thirty minutes to get a new canvas in here."

A cheer went up from the crowd, and Tinto looked a little happier.

"I think we've seen enough of this miracle, don't you?" said Mr. Sears to the class. "Now then, is everyone wearing a wristwatch today, like I asked? Good. Does everyone have the right time? Excellent. Then you're all free to visit the animal you've chosen to write about on your next report. Study its behavior. Take as many notes as you can. I want details, people! You've got half an hour, starting now. We'll meet again by the flagpole. When? That's right, in half an hour. All right, people, let's go!"

The Hargrove contingent broke up into groups and

ran off like wilder animals than those in any of the zoo habitats.

Lila looked around and spotted her dad, who was talking to the zoo official. She went over and joined them.

"I thought we had an extra canvas," the zoo official was saying apologetically. "But I guess we don't, after all. What about the one Tinto smashed? Do you think you can mend it? He stepped all over it, but we can probably wash off the dirt and hay with a hose."

"Thanks for your help," Lila's dad told her calmly. "Perhaps we can arrange another painting session with Tinto soon."

"You got it," said the zoo official.

"Come here, sweetie," Lila's dad said to Lila. "Give your dad a hug. His gallery just lost a Tinto masterpiece."

Lila hugged her dad and said she was sorry about it. Then she added, "I wouldn't take it too hard, Dad. I don't think Tinto really put all of his talent into that one anyway."

Her dad laughed and said, "You're probably right, sweetie. I know you have another report to do. Don't let me take up any more of your valuable time. I'm okay now. I've recovered from the shock of my loss."

"My zoo report is going to be on the North American Gray Wolf or Timber Wolf, *Canis lupus,*" said Lila. "It's the same animal I chose to report on in the Red Level, the Green Level, the Orange Level, and the Blue Level. I pretty much know the subject backward and forward already."

"Well, try to discover something new," said her dad. "I'll

meet you over there after I call the gallery and tell them the bad news about Tinto's smashed masterpiece. I'm going to have to break it to them gently."

He took out his cell phone, and Lila headed off to the wolf habitat. It had rained earlier, but the sky was now sunny and clear. The air smelled fresh, even with all of the various animal odors floating around.

Lila loved the smells of animals, even the unpleasant ones. She had wanted to be a veterinarian for as long as she could remember. Even without training, she had already successfully nursed several wounded animals back to health. Just recently, she had released a pigeon whose injured wing she had bandaged, and her heart had soared as high as the bird did when it finally flew away. Nothing would make her happier than to care for animals on a daily basis. Every time she came to the zoo it struck her how many different types of them were in the world, and the thought that she might learn to help them all one day made her very happy and excited indeed.

But there were some problems even a veterinarian couldn't fix, she thought with a roll of her eyes. No veterinarian could cure Tinto the genius painter elephant of being a show-off, for example. The only cure for that was a lot more humiliation in front of a crowd.

The first thing Lila noticed as she approached the wolf habitat was the large Alpha Female sitting on a soggy piece of carpet on the grass.

Oh great, she thought, another show-off!

And then she caught sight of a bright red head of hair.

Her heart began to beat very fast.

That's another sign, she thought excitedly. I obviously wouldn't get this worked up over a total stranger, would I?

She ran up to Callum and hugged him impulsively.

"Clam! There you are! I'm so glad you're safe," she told him. "Although I still want to sue that stupid Billy Bankson for every cent he's got!"

"Well, looky here," said a man who was standing nearby. He had a camera slung around his neck. There was something horribly wrong with his nose, Lila noticed, but she was polite enough to ignore it. "Another Firehead!" he said. "I'd recognize your sister anywhere, Clam. You could be twins, as a matter of fact. Fraternal, not identical, of course. How do you do, little lady? My name is Buzz Optigon. Yep, the world-famous wildlife wrangler."

"How do you do," said Lila. "But Clam isn't my brother. I mean, not that I know of. Still, I'd like to ask him some questions. Where'd you get the name Firehead?" she said, asking Callum point-blank.

"From Grampa," Callum replied truthfully.

"Which Grampa?" asked Lila. "The one on your dad's side of the family or your mom's?"

Callum thought about it. Grampa was always bragging that Dad was his son.

"On my dad's," he said finally.

"Oh," said Lila, sounding crestfallen. "Then you can't be my brother after all. Because my grampa on my dad's side of the family died before I was born. He was golfing in Scotland when it started to rain, and he and his Australian caddie were swallowed up by a sand trap that had suddenly turned into quicksand."

"Quicksand is nasty stuff, all right," agreed Buzz with a shudder. "I've had a few close calls with it myself. I lost two of my best cameras that way. But never on a golf course. That's a new one to me."

Just then, Lila's dad came running up, all out of breath.

"*What? How?*" he cried excitedly, taking Callum by the shoulders and giving him a shake, as if to make sure that he was real and not just a figment of his overworked imagination.

"Another fan," said Buzz, trying to sound modest. "I've got a million of 'em. Buzz Optigon, sir, at your service."

"*Do you know who this is?*" Lila's dad asked Lila, after hugging Callum so tightly that it looked as though he were going to squeeze him to death.

"Hold on, Dad," said Lila. "This is Clam Firehead. Remember? The new kid I told you about. He got his last name from his grampa. The one on his *dad's* side of the family."

"His grampa?" said Lila's dad. "I don't understand."

Lila thought for a moment. Then she looked Callum in

the eye and said, "Listen carefully, Clam. Was your grampa a man, like Dad and Buzz?"

Callum shook his head slowly. He pointed to the sign that said: NORTH AMERICAN GRAY WOLF OR TIMBER WOLF, CANIS LUPUS.

"Grampa was one of these guys," he said frankly. "And so were the rest of the family."

"Well, I'll be," said Buzz in awe. "That's the best wolf whisperer I ever saw, right there!"

"This boy is my son," Lila's dad said to Buzz, his eyes misting over with tears. "There's no doubt about it. I should know. I've been searching for him for years." He took Callum by the shoulders again and looked him straight in the eye, just as Lila had done. "Do you know me? I'm your dad," he said lovingly. "And this is Lila, your twin sister. Fraternal, not identical. We've finally found you again after all these years. Do you understand what I'm saying, son? You're not Clam Firehead."

"I'm not?" Callum asked. He didn't mind. He was never all that hot on that name anyway.

"No," said his real dad. "You're Callum Throckmorton!"

Callum was thunderstruck. The sound of his name was like a key that fit into the lock at the back of his mind, and the shadowy figures were suddenly as clear as could be.

They were his mom and dad. And Lila. The last time he saw them, they were driving away from the campsite in the woods long ago, leaving him behind, doomed to face the dangers of the Wild alone and unprotected.

But he wasn't mad at them anymore, let alone furious. He was positively ecstatic to see them again!

CHAPTER NINETEEN
A Family Reunion

Mr. Throckmorton could not wait to hear all about how Callum had found his way to the city. He had him tell his story right there, in front of the Gray Wolf or Timber Wolf (*Canis lupus*) habitat.

"God bless all kind and considerate people who help poor souls in need!" he cried when Callum had gotten to the part about Mrs. T-G and Mr. O'Malley and all they had done for him, putting him on the train and getting rid of his head lice and everything.

Ew, thought Lila disgustedly. I guess there are some animals I don't like after all.

At the very start of Callum's story, a small group of zoo visitors had stopped to hear it, and by the time he had finished, a big crowd had gathered. It seemed that people were looking for any kind of excitement after Tinto the genius painter elephant's new masterpiece had proved such a bust.

"That's the most touching story I ever heard, minus the part about ripping a caribou to bits," said one zoo visitor, dabbing her eyes.

"If only Tinto the genius painter elephant had a new canvas right now," said another zoo visitor. "He could paint a picture about it."

"Come on, guys," said Mr. Throckmorton, putting his arms around Lila and Callum. "We're going home. Lila, run ahead and tell Mr. Sears that I'm taking you out of school for the rest of the day."

"Hooray!" she said.

"Wait a minute," interrupted a voice from the crowd of zoo visitors. A big, burly man in a dark blue uniform stepped forward.

Callum recognized the uniform right away. It was another police officer. I'm in for it now, he thought anxiously.

"Listen, mac, that girl may be your daughter," the police officer told Mr. Throckmorton, "but you've got no hard proof that this boy is related to you. I heard the whole story, and there's not one solid fact to back it up. I say we all go down to the station and let the chief of police decide what to do with the matter."

"*Not on your life, officer!*" Mr. Throckmorton fairly shouted. "*I'm taking my son home with me, and you're going to let me do it!*"

Wow, thought Callum admiringly. There's a true Alpha Male for you!

"I'm glad I have my camera," said Buzz, who was equally impressed, as he snapped a shot.

"Well, all right, then," the police officer said obligingly. "I'll let you go just this once." He was used to taking orders.

Mr. Throckmorton put a protective arm around each of his children and guided them quickly through the crowd. Wait, thought Callum, I didn't say good-bye to Buzz. But when he turned around to look for him, the world-famous wildlife wrangler was nowhere in sight.

Mrs. Throckmorton was already home when Mr. Throckmorton, Lila, and Callum walked in the front door.

"I don't believe my eyes!" she cried when she saw Callum, and it was probably true, since her eyes were so filled with happy tears that it was hard for her to see anything clearly.

She rushed at her long-lost offspring and gathered him up in her arms. "It's Mom, Callum, honey," she said through her sobs. "I've missed you so much. Welcome home!"

All at once Callum felt his heart grow tight, and it didn't seem that he could breathe anymore. He grew dizzy. The room began to spin. It was all too much for him. He knew this woman! She was his mom! He knew that man! He was his dad! He knew Lila. She was his twin sister, fraternal, not identical!

This was his family.

His *real* family.

This was where he *belonged*.

The room stopped spinning. His heart didn't feel tight

anymore. He could breathe again. He started to smile, and then he couldn't stop smiling.

"Are you hungry, honey?" asked his mom. "Of course you are! You must be starving. What would you like? Anything special?"

"Something rotten and diseased," he said.

"He's a carnivore," said Lila happily.

"I'm going to make you the most rotten and diseased thing you've ever tasted," said his mom.

I've got the best mom in the whole world, thought Callum.

"And while I'm making you a bite to eat, honey," said his mom, "I want you to go upstairs and take a bath. Nothing personal, sweetheart, but you smell absolutely atrocious. Lila, go up and show your brother how to draw the bathwater, please. Throw in lots and lots of my special lilac bath crystals. And tell him to pass his clothes through the door. They need washing too. Callum, I don't think we have any clothes in the house that will fit you, but until these clothes are washed and dried, you can wear one of your dad's terrycloth robes."

To Mr. Throckmorton, she said, "Dear, you're going to have to go out and do a little emergency shopping. We'll need a pair of jeans and some T-shirts to start with, and some new underwear."

She checked the tags on Callum's borrowed shirt and pants and wrote down the sizes. "Run along upstairs now," she told Callum and Lila. "We'll eat in a jiffy."

Upstairs, Lila showed Callum the bathtub and how to use the faucets and adjust the water temperature. She poured plenty of her mom's lilac bath crystals into the hot, swirling water. Then she showed him the sponge, the scrub brush, and the soap, and explained how to use them. Finally she took out a big fluffy towel that he could dry himself off with when he was done washing.

"Lila?" he said shyly. "I'm sorry I ran off with Billy that day and all. I didn't mean to hurt your feelings."

"Forget about it," she said generously. "I forgive you. Now take off your clothes and pass them through the door. Don't worry, I won't look."

Soon Callum had settled down in the tub amid the lilac-scented bubbles. Then he picked up the sponge, the scrub brush, and the soap, and scrubbed his arms and legs, his feet and hands, the back of his neck, his back (as far as he could reach), and his chest and stomach. By the time he was finished, the fluffy white lilac-scented bubbles were the color of a mud puddle, and his skin was glowing pink.

I'm a new person now, he thought with satisfaction. But I smell a little flowery!

His stomach rumbled, and he hoped that Mom had finished making him something rotten and diseased to eat. He got out of the tub and dried himself off with the big fluffy towel. He found one of Dad's terry-cloth robes hanging on the handle on the other side of the bathroom door. The sleeves had been rolled up to fit him better. It was soft and comfy.

He hurried downstairs and joined Lila and Mom in the kitchen. Mom got happy tears in her eyes again when she saw him.

"You smell so much better now, honey," she said gladly. "I just love those lilac crystals. Sit down at the table. I made you a ham and cheese omelet with a side of bacon and tomato slices. I hope it's rotten and diseased enough for you. I know it's already time for lunch, but I always make breakfast in the mornings, and you've got a lot of catching up to do."

"I'm having lunch," said Lila. "A tomato and tomato sandwich."

"A vegetarian and a carnivore eating together in peace, side by side," Mom said approvingly. "It's a beautiful thing."

Just then, Mr. Throckmorton rushed through the door, carrying two enormous department store bags. "*He's still here!*" he cried, sounding ecstatic and relieved all at the same time.

"Of course he's still here, dear," said Mrs. Throckmorton. "You aren't going away ever again, are you, Callum?"

Callum shook his head vigorously, his mouth full of rotten and diseased deliciousness.

"And we're never going to lose you again," Mom and Dad promised firmly. "We're going to keep you right here in the family, where you belong. We've never stopped needing you, and wanting you, and loving you!"

This is a real change for the better, Callum thought happily. This pack actually wants me, for once!

"I got you ten pairs of jeans and seventeen T-shirts," said Dad, setting the two enormous department store bags on the table. "And thirty-two pairs of underwear and twenty-three pairs of socks."

"Good gracious," said Mom. "We're taking most of that back. But you're free to change into one pair of jeans, one T-shirt, one pair of underwear, and one pair of socks when you're finished, honey. And let's all thank Dad for being so generous and for taking the rest of these clothes back for a refund."

"Thanks, Dad," said Lila.

Callum stopped chewing in midbite, a look of alarm on his face.

"What's wrong, honey?" Mom asked, concerned. "Don't you *want* to wear clothes? I'm afraid you have to. The neighbors expect it. You're back in Civilization now. You're not living in the Wild anymore."

But he wasn't worried about that. It was something he had forgotten; something closer to home. He lowered his head reverently over his plate of food.

"Oh Great Spirit that guides the Sun and Moon and Lights the Stars and watches over All That Lives in This World and Beyond," he said, "I thank You for this nourishing meal, although You had less to do with it than Mom did this time."

Now that he was so good at speaking, it was no surprise that he said the whole thing without making a single mistake.

"It was nothing, really," Mom said modestly. "I couldn't have done it without the Great Spirit."

Lila lowered her head too.

"Dear Great Spirit," she said. "What Callum said goes for me too. Thank you for my tomato sandwich."

"Amen to that," said Mr. Throckmorton respectfully.

Half a minute later Callum's plate was licked clean. "That's what I like to see," said Mom. "A good healthy appetite. Only no tongues on the dishes, please. It's a house rule."

"There are lots of those," Lila told Callum confidentially. "I'll tell you about them later."

Then Mom let him pick out some clothes from the two enormous department store bags and said, "Run along and change, honey, then come back downstairs and we'll have a nice talk."

Callum took his new clothes and raced upstairs, taking the steps two at a time.

"Walk up the stairs, honey!" called Mom. "We never run indoors. That's another house rule!"

Then she said to Lila, "Remind me to get an extra tooth-brush out of the drawer, will you, sweetie? He can have the room next to yours for a bedroom, the way we always intended. Oh my gosh! He's got to see the dentist right away. And he's got to go to the doctor for a complete and thorough checkup."

Wow, thought Lila sympathetically. My newfound brother is in for a lot of fun.

Mr. Throckmorton took out a piece of notebook paper and started to write down all of the things that needed to be done now that Callum was back in the family. "We'll have to get that old camping equipment out of the room next to Lila's, and then we'll have to move a bed in there," he said eagerly. "I don't know where to start! There's so much to do!"

Just then the doorbell rang.

"Who on earth can that be, I wonder?" he complained. "Just when we're making a list of all of the things that need to be done before we can live our lives a minute longer!"

"It's your sister, dear, and her husband," said Mrs. Throckmorton. "I invited them over. I didn't tell them why. I thought we ought to break the news to them gently."

Break it to them gently, thought Lila. Like Dad did with the gallery after Tinto the genius painter elephant smashed his masterpiece. To blurt everything out right away would be too great a shock.

"Lila, honey, go open the door for Aunt Donaldina and Uncle Luther, please," said Mom. "Tell them that Dad and I will be there in a sec."

"Hi, Aunt Donaldina, hi, Uncle Luther," said Lila as she opened the door. "Mom and Dad will be here in a sec."

"Lila, darling, *what* in *heaven's name* is the *big mystery?*" demanded Aunt Donaldina as she swept into the room, the hem of her long fake-fur coat flapping behind her.

"Nice to see you again, Lila, sweetheart," said her uncle

Luther. "You look cute as a button in your school uniform."

Lila looked down at what she was wearing and saw the navy blue Hargrove Academy blazer. Well, what do you know? she thought in surprise. I haven't gotten around to changing out of my school clothes yet! She usually changed right away.

"Hi, Donaldina, hi, Luther," said Mr. and Mrs. Throckmorton, coming into the room.

"*Not* another *word,* dears," said Aunt Donaldina. "I *insist* that you *spill the beans.* Luther and I are headed off to the city offices of the Forestry Service to discuss the *land bequest* for our proposed *wildlife sanctuary.* I'm afraid we've hit a *snag.*"

"Oh dear," said Mr. and Mrs. Throckmorton. "Not a snag."

"It's just a technicality," said Uncle Luther calmly. "We'll get over it. I've never lost a case."

"Well," said Mrs. Throckmorton, "the reason we've asked you here is because something rather unusual happened at the zoo today."

"It's *what's his name,* that *ridiculous* genius painter elephant, isn't it?" asked Aunt Donaldina, giving her brother a sisterly frown. "I warned you about that, Campbell. I *told* you that a *genius painter elephant* sounded *too good* to be *true.* I suppose the gallery has found out that he's an *absolute fake* and they're *suing* you for *every cent you've got,* and you want Luther to save the day for you *again.* Can you fit that into your schedule, Luther, dear?"

"Probably," said Uncle Luther complacently. "Let me check."

"No, no, it's nothing like that," said Mr. Throckmorton hurriedly. "Tinto is really quite a talented painter, for an elephant. I don't know if he's a genius like some people say, but he manages to hit the blank canvas with his broom more often than not."

"He's just a little clumsy sometimes," said Lila, "and accidentally smashes his masterpiece. And he doesn't seem to take his talent very seriously."

"That's a very perceptive analysis, Lila," said Mr. Throckmorton, and she smiled proudly. "No, what happened at the zoo today was something else entirely, Donaldina. To make a long story short, we found Callum. That is, Lila and I did."

"I found him first," said Lila, even more proudly.

"I don't understand," said Aunt Donaldina. "You found *Callum*? Callum *who*?"

"Callum Throckmorton," said Mr. Throckmorton. "*Our* Callum."

"*Good gracious!*" cried Aunt Donaldina. "I thought that *subject* was *closed*. Are you *sure* it's *him*?"

"More importantly," said Uncle Luther, "will it stand up in court?"

"Absolutely," said Mr. Throckmorton. "In fact, here he is."

He turned toward Callum, who had come down the stairs. He looked very presentable in his new jeans and T-shirt.

"Hi again," said Callum to Aunt Donaldina.

"What the ...? How the ...? Why, I never!" cried Aunt Donaldina. *"It's Clam, like the mollusk! This news is too much for me! Someone, bring me a soda!"*

"Lila, bring your Aunt Donaldina a soda, please," said Mrs. Throckmorton.

"Diet or regular?" asked Lila.

"Regular!" cried Aunt Donaldina, throwing caution to the wind.

"I don't understand," said Mr. Throckmorton confusedly. "Do you two know each other?"

"Dad, this is Mrs. T-G," said Callum. "I told you about her, remember? She helped me get on the train and she got me something rotten and diseased to eat. I'm sorry I never said thank you for that, Mrs. T-G. I was kind of confused at that point. I didn't know which end was up."

"You've lost your accent!" cried Mrs. T-G in shock.

"You are *Mrs. T-G?"* cried Mr. Throckmorton, staring at his sister as if he'd never seen her before. "Of course!" he then said, smacking his forehead. "Mrs. Throckmorton-Gordon."

"I *got* him that *haircut!"* cried Aunt Donaldina emotionally. "I *cured* him of *head lice!"*

Actually, it was Mr. O'Malley who did that, thought Callum. And does she *really* have to bring up the head lice again?

"Luther, please call and cancel our meeting with the Forestry Service," Mrs. T-G went on excitedly. "This is a *family reunion*. We must stay for supper!"

"Sounds good," said Uncle Luther, reaching for his cell phone.

"I thought you'd say that," said Mrs. Throckmorton with a gracious smile. "I figure we'll have spaghetti with meatballs."

"Yuck," said Lila.

"Disgusting," said Aunt Donaldina.

"Yum!" said Callum.

"Sounds delicious!" said Mr. Throckmorton and Uncle Luther.

"And spaghetti with vegetarian marinara sauce," added Mrs. Throckmorton.

"Yum!" said Lila.

"Sounds delicious!" said Aunt Donaldina, looking at Uncle Luther severely.

"I'll have a little of both," he said diplomatically.

During dinner everyone had a million questions for Callum, and he told nearly a gazillion stories about the time that he spent with the pack and the predator lifestyle, although Mom was forced to say, "Please, honey, not while we're eating," whenever he described something especially gross, like the savage ripping and tearing that went on after a kill.

"*Oh* my *stars*," cried Aunt Donaldina, putting her hands to her throat. "I'll never look at a *caribou* the same way *again*."

"Maybe that's what your wildlife sanctuary can be for, Donaldina," suggested Mr. Throckmorton. "To protect all those poor animals from predators."

"Oh, no," she said firmly. "We can't interfere with the laws of Nature. And no one can say for certain that we will even *have* a sanctuary at this point, I'm afraid. There's a catch."

"Is that the snag?" asked Lila, trying to get the terms straight.

"Exactly," sighed Aunt Donaldina.

"Like I said before, it's just a technicality," said Uncle Luther as calmly as ever. "It shouldn't be a problem. I've never lost a case. Please pass the meatballs again. They're ever so delish."

"What kind of technicality is it?" asked Mrs. Throckmorton.

"We are required to put the land to special use," replied Aunt Donaldina. "And we don't have a clue about how to do that."

"What does special use mean?" asked Callum.

"It means that we've got to use our sanctuary to help Nature's creatures in some *special* way if we want it to exist at all," said Aunt Donaldina. "And it doesn't have to be wildlife. *Any* life will do."

"You mean you can start a chinchilla farm?" asked Mr. Throckmorton, helping himself to more meatballs too.

"*Certainly not*," said Aunt Donaldina, sounding horrified.

"You mean it's got to be like a home for endangered species?" asked Lila, helping herself to more vegetarian marinara sauce.

"*Yes*," said Aunt Donaldina. "It could *definitely* be something like that. Whatever it is, though, we've got to act quickly. The deadline for our proposal is early next week."

Callum chewed his diseased and rotten spaghetti thoughtfully.

He had listened, and he'd caught every word.

Especially Lila's.

And his instinct told him that he had found a way of contributing something useful to the pack.

CHAPTER TWENTY
Callum and Lila's Grand Plan

Callum spent his first night in his own bedroom, and there wasn't even a bed in it. He lay snuggled up in an old musty sleeping bag on top of a leaky air mattress, and he couldn't have been happier.

Lila's room was right next door. Just before bedtime they looked at a few of the books on her shelves. "Do you remember these? Mom and Dad used to read them to us," she said and showed him all sorts of big, colorful books on nature and insects and animals in the wild. And suddenly he remembered them, word for word. Especially a big brown book called *Wolves and Their Ways*, which was filled with pictures and diagrams of Alphas and Betas and Omegas and the things that they did. Now that he had firsthand experience, he could tell that the writer of the book had got it pretty right.

With the excitement of the day, it was hard not to fall

asleep as soon as his head hit the pillow, but he had some serious thinking to do. Although he couldn't see it, the moon was high in the sky by the time he finally allowed himself to drift off into dreamland.

"Come on, you two!" Mom called up the stairs late the next morning. "Quit that yakking and come downstairs! Breakfast is waiting!"

Then, when Lila and Callum were finally seated at the breakfast table, she said, "Honestly. You two have all the time in the world to get to know each other again. You don't have to do it all in one morning."

"We were just saying how much we'd like Aunt Donaldina and Uncle Luther to come over again for dinner tonight," said Lila.

Callum smiled at her. She smiled back.

"That's very sweet of you guys," said Dad, sighing over his only slice of bacon as if it were a piece of solid gold, same as he did every morning. "But your aunt and uncle are busy people, especially with this whole sanctuary snag that they've got on their hands. They may have other plans."

"Then we'll just have to beg them," said Lila. "Because we really want to see them tonight."

"Yes, it sure sounds like it," said Dad. "Okay, I'll call them up and ask them over."

"*Hooray!*" yelled Lila and Callum.

"No shouting at the table," said Dad. "It's a house rule, remember?"

"I keep forgetting about that one," said Lila to Callum.

"What's going on with you two?" Mom asked. "You seem to be hatching a grand plan or something. Do you care to enlighten your loving parents as to what it is, or do you want to keep us in the dark?"

Lila and Callum only looked at each other and giggled.

"In the dark it is, then," said Dad, who didn't sound very concerned about being left out of the loop. "I don't mind. At least I've got my lovely wife for company."

"And I've got my lovely husband," said Mom, who didn't sound very concerned about it either.

Now that they had their family back together again, they were so happy that even if they stubbed their toes on the stairs or something painful like that, they'd probably still be smiling.

"What's on our agendas for today?" asked Dad.

"School!" cried Lila excitedly. "And if I don't get a move on, I'm going to be late. May I be excused from the table?"

"You may," said Mom.

"Callum and I have school today too, sort of," said Dad. "We're meeting with Ms. Mendez at the Hargrove Academy to see what can be done about educating a certain Wild Boy who has never attended a full day of school in his life."

"He's got a lot of homework to catch up on, that's for sure!" Lila yelled from the stairs.

"No yelling from the stairs!" yelled Dad. *"That's another house rule!"*

Then he turned to Mom and asked, "And what are you up to today, dear?"

"Well," said Mom, "I did some more thinking last night about the bossasaurus skeleton, and I decided that the arm bone that I thought was a leg bone is an arm bone after all . . ."

"The head bone's connected to the neck bone," Dad started singing. "The neck bone's connected to the . . ."

"Stomach bone?" offered Callum, and Mom and Dad laughed, but not in a mean way.

"That's pretty close, son," said Dad. "We'll work on it. I'll bring home an anatomy diagram."

"So I'm going to switch the bone back to where I had it in the first place, and then go on from there," Mom went on. "But that won't take all day. I thought I'd take the afternoon off and meet up with you guys and we could do something fun."

"I'd like to go to the park," said Callum.

"That would be fun," said Mom.

"I'd like that too," said Dad.

"Like what?" asked Lila, coming back into the kitchen with her hair newly combed and her teeth freshly brushed.

"Callum and Mom and I are going to the park this afternoon after Mom gets off work," Dad told her.

"Good job!" Lila said to Callum, and Callum looked pleased.

"Something is definitely going on with you two," said

Mom, narrowing her eyes. "I feel like I'm in a spy movie this morning. I hope you're not planning to steal any state secrets. I'd hate to have to flee the country before I've figured out this whole arm bone/leg bone problem with my bossasaurus skeleton."

"I second that," said Dad. "No stealing any state secrets. Let's all have a happy and productive day. We'll rendezvous back here around six o'clock tonight and touch base at dinner."

Callum and Dad spent the next hour or so packing dusty camping equipment into cardboard boxes, and then they took a cab to the Hargrove Academy for the Gifted, Bright, and Perceptive Child to meet with Ms. Mendez.

As it happened, Ms. Mendez was so busy that she couldn't see them right away, but after waiting for a while on a hard wooden bench outside her office, they were ushered inside.

The walls of her office were crowded with shiny diplomas and certificates and testimonials all praising the benefits of a Hargrove education. The shelves were jammed with glittering trophies showing that the gifted, bright, and perceptive Hargrove student could kick butt on the basketball court, at the track meet, and on the soccer field as well as in the classroom. And Ms. Mendez's desk was piled high with forms and papers and documents, which showed that she was very important too.

She was a sharp-eyed, neatly dressed person, and she reminded Callum of a little nervous bird, like the kind that was always hopping on the ground under the pretzel vendor's cart at the zoo, hoping to pick up a crumb here and there.

"Ah, Mr. Throckmorton," she began, peering over an open folder. "Lila's father. We do so appreciate having Lila here at Hargrove. She is a credit to the Hargrove way of life. We expect great things from her, and we're certain she will not disappoint us."

"Thank you," said Dad. "I'm certain about that too. Lila has never disappointed anybody."

"And this must be Callum," Ms. Mendez went on, looking decidedly less pleased. "Although he was with us for less than a day under dubious circumstances, he managed to get an innocent Hargrove student into trouble with the law."

"I don't believe Billy Bankson was innocent on that day or any other," said Dad firmly, who knew all the facts. "And I think that you should keep in mind that Callum is a special case. He has only just begun to relearn the ways of Civilization. The rules and regulations that you and I know so well are all Greek to him. He's been living in the Wild, in the company of wolves, until only recently. In point of fact, he was raised by wolves."

"Callum?" asked Ms. Mendez in disbelief. "Raised by wolves?"

"Exactly," said Dad. "And so you see, he's only now learning the many things that you and I take for granted. And one of the things that he's learned is not to make friends with a bully like Billy Bankson. We're here today to see how the Hargrove Academy can contribute to educating him to the grade level where he would be if he *weren't* raised by wolves, which would be Lila's grade, since she is his twin sister, fraternal, not identical. By which I mean the Yellow Level."

"I see," said Ms. Mendez coldly. "Well, Mr. Throckmorton, all I can tell you is that I will take the matter under consideration. And now I think we're done here. You may be excused."

"Thank you, Ms. Mendez," said Callum and Dad politely.

"Don't worry," Dad told Callum in the cab to the park afterward. "If push comes to shove, we'll sic Uncle Luther on her. He's never lost a case."

"Okay, Dad," said Callum, filled with admiration. His dad was a total Alpha, through and through. He could do no wrong.

They got out of the cab a couple of blocks ahead of the park so that they could get cherry colas to drink on the way. Sipping their sodas, they turned the corner and saw a few tipped-over trash cans. Disgusting garbage littered the street.

"Yuck," said Dad, picking a path around it. "Let's not step in any of that."

A little farther down the street, they came upon two mangy mongrels looking hungry and scared.

"There are so many stray dogs in the city," said Dad sympathetically. "If only something could be done to help them."

Callum was less sympathetic. "What's the matter with you?" he asked the dogs in the language of the Wild, sounding as stern as Ms. Mendez had been to his dad and him earlier. "Haven't you heard? You're supposed to clean up the mess you make after you tip over a trash can!"

The dogs perked up at this and then they looked ashamed, although just as hungry.

"I'll be darned," said Dad to Callum. "Where'd you learn to bark like that? Oh . . . *right*."

Wincing, he devoted himself to draining the last precious drops of cherry cola from his can, as Callum said a few more things to the strays that sounded a lot like instructions. The dogs grinned like crazy and wagged their tails like mad, and then ran off with a purpose.

It was a glorious day in the park. A group of friends were throwing a Frisbee on the lawn. Others were having a picnic under the big, sprawling, leafy trees. Mothers were out walking their babies and toddlers in baby carriages and strollers, and various other people were happily milling around.

None of the mothers was the one Callum and Billy had frightened nearly out of her wits the other day, Callum was relieved to see.

There was an open area with a few tables and seats set in concrete. On various tabletops, chessboards and checkerboards had been painted so that anyone who brought their own game pieces could play. Grouped around one of the chessboard tables were the three Grampas that Callum had befriended at the illegal campfire the night he left Billy's smelly den to get some fresh air.

Callum brought Dad over to meet them.

"Er . . . where are we going, Callum?" asked Dad, a little confused.

"I'd like you to meet some friends of mine," he said. "Tom, Dick, and Harry."

"You're kidding me," said Dad.

The three Grampas were arguing over the game of chess they were playing. In place of the usual chessmen, they were using twigs and rocks and the odd nut or two.

"You're cheating!" Tom complained to Dick. "That acorn was a pawn a moment ago, and now you're telling me it's a knight!"

"That acorn has *always* been a knight," retorted Dick. "Unlike your green twig, which has switched from a rook to a bishop three times already."

"Why don't you two play checkers instead?" suggested Harry. "Sticks can play black, and stones can play red. There's no confusing that."

Then all three of them looked up and noticed Callum.

"Holy guacamole!" cried Tom. "Look who it is! Clam, like the mollusk!"

"As I live and breathe!" cried Dick. "Which isn't too well lately, I'm afraid."

"It's good to see you, son," said Harry. "We were worried about you. We thought quicksand had swallowed you up or something. You never can tell where you're going to find quicksand these days. I've heard a lot of strange stories."

"Hi, guys," said Callum. "It turns out that my name is Callum, not Clam. It's not at all like the mollusk."

"That makes more sense," said Dick.

Then the three Grampas noticed Mr. Throckmorton.

"Oh, drat!" cried Tom. "The kid's with the law! He's brought an undercover cop with him! City shelter, here we come."

"We have every right to play chess, even with unauthorized game pieces," Dick protested, getting riled.

"And we stopped gambling ten minutes ago," declared Harry.

"No, no," said Mr. Throckmorton. "It's nothing like that. I'm Mr. Throckmorton, Callum's father."

"Some father!" snorted Tom.

"You call yourself a father?" scowled Dick.

"What kind of a father lets his kid run around all alone in the park in the middle of the night?" scolded Harry.

Mr. Throckmorton was so ashamed that he didn't have the nerve to confess to the Grampas that he had actually done far worse than that by leaving Callum to fend for himself in the Wild as a toddler.

"Don't blame my dad," Callum said, standing up for him with Beta fury. "He had nothing to do with me running around all alone in the park that night. He thought I had vanished from the face of the earth, and I didn't even know he existed. He was just a shadowy figure at the back of my mind at that point."

"My apologies then," said Tom.

"I take it all back," said Dick.

"Forgive me, if you can," said Harry.

"Think nothing of it," said Mr. Throckmorton, who was glad to have gotten off so lightly.

"I'm the one who's sorry," said Callum to the three Grampas. "I shouldn't have run out on you guys in your hour of need that night by the campfire."

"That's okay," said the Grampas. "It turns out the city shelter wasn't as bad as we thought. They've invested in some air fresheners."

"How would you like to come to my den—I mean, my house for dinner tonight?" Callum asked them.

"Er . . . ," said Mr. Throckmorton uneasily.

"That is, if it's all right with my dad," said Callum. "Is it, Dad? Can my three friends come to dinner?"

"Of course they can," said Mr. Throckmorton grandly. "But remember, we've invited Aunt Donaldina and Uncle Luther too."

"Well, I never," said Tom, surprised as anything.

"I don't know what to say," said Dick.

"What's the address?" said Harry. "I'm always up for a bite."

"Thanks for letting my friends come to dinner, Dad," said Callum as the two of them were walking back through the park.

"No problem," said Mr. Throckmorton. "We'll just have

to break it to your Mom gently. I told her that we'd meet her by the flagpole at the zoo. I want to look in on Tinto the genius painter elephant while we're here."

"That's perfect," said Callum happily.

"I don't know what you're up to," said Dad, "but please don't tell me. It's so peaceful being in the dark."

They met Mom by the flagpole at the zoo right on time. She smiled bravely when Dad informed her about the three strange gentlemen who were coming to dinner, and then she said it would be fine. "Good thing we're having tacos," she said. "They're easy and fun, and they go a long way."

Dad hurried off to check on Tinto the genius painter elephant. Apparently, Tinto was in a real funk over something and wouldn't even look at a blank canvas.

"What can you do?" Dad said philosophically. "Artists have their moods. I'll see what I can do to spark his creative spirit. I'll try not to be away too long. Have fun."

"What now, honey?" Mom asked Callum. "Is there anything in particular you want to do?" and Callum led her to the little cabin where Buzz Optigon was staying.

"What is this place, honey?" Mom asked a little worriedly.

"You'll see," said Callum.

They knocked on the door, and Buzz answered it. "So, the time has finally come. I figured you'd be knocking on my door sooner or later," he said to Callum. Then he noticed

Mrs. Throckmorton. "I suppose this is your lawyer," he said. "Go ahead. Sue me for every cent I've got. It was worth it, I tell you. Worth it!"

Callum was confused. But then, he thought, so was Buzz.

"This isn't my lawyer," he said. "This is my mom."

"How do you do," said Mrs. Throckmorton politely, who had been waiting to be introduced.

"Sorry, ma'am," said Buzz. "My mistake."

"What was worth it?" Callum asked Buzz.

Buzz eyed him suspiciously. "You mean you really don't know?" he asked.

"*Know what?*" demanded Callum and Mom, who had really had enough of this mystery by now.

"Come inside," said Buzz. "Both of you." He led Callum and Mrs. Throckmorton to the small kitchen. On the small table was one of the glossy supermarket tabloid magazines that usually feature such outlandish stories as aliens from outer space meeting with the United Nations to discuss world peace.

The headline on the cover screamed WOLF BOY REUNITED WITH FAMILY AT ZOO. Underneath that it said EXCLUSIVE STORY BY WORLD-FAMOUS WILDLIFE WRANGLER BUZZ OPTIGON. And there was a printed photo of Dad and Callum and Lila looking all misty-eyed, taken at the very moment they had been reunited.

"I couldn't help myself," Buzz said somewhat shame-facedly. "The story was too good to resist. It's a good photo, isn't it? Probably the first I ever took where the subject wasn't trying to bite my head off."

"You're Buzz Optigon?" said Mrs. Throckmorton admiringly. "I've heard of you. We've got all your books at home. I thought you were ripped to pieces by a rampaging horde of rhesus monkeys in the Himalaya Mountains."

"So did a lot of people," said Buzz with chagrin. "But not anymore. Thanks to this article, everyone who's anyone will know I'm still alive. I'd give you an autograph, but my sapsucker injuries are acting up again."

"I'm not here about the article," said Callum. "But congratulations anyway."

"Thanks," said Buzz proudly. "I did a good job on it."

"I'm here to ask you to come to dinner at my house tonight," Callum went on. "We've having tacos."

"Er . . . ," said Mrs. Throckmorton uneasily.

"That is, if it's okay with my mom," said Callum. "Is it, Mom? Can my friend come to dinner?"

"Of course he can," said Mrs. Throckmorton grandly. "We'll just have to break it to your dad gently."

"I'd be happy to come," said Buzz. "I love tacos."

"Great," said Callum. "See you then."

Lila was waiting for them when Mom and Dad and Callum returned home. "I know I should have waited to ask your permission first," she told Mom and Dad, "but I invited Becca Adams, Rachel Cohen, Curtis Takahashi, and Tito Jones to dinner with us tonight."

"Fine," said Dad.

"Why not?" said Mom. "We've invited half the city already anyway, so four more won't make any difference." Then she said to Dad, "I wrote out the shopping list this morning. Just get triple of everything. I'll go next door to the Bahramis and borrow their folding chairs."

Then she said to Callum and Lila, "You're not fooling anyone, you know. We realize this is all part of your grand plan. I just hope I can survive whatever it is you've got in store for us."

And so it was that when everyone sat down at the dinner table that night, there were fourteen chairs around the table and fourteen people sitting there. Since hardly anyone knew anyone else, there were a lot of questions asked and answered and a lot of time spent getting to know one another. When everyone had eaten enough tacos and salad and drunk enough cherry cola, Callum and Lila stood up to make an announcement.

"Callum and I are glad that you could all make it here tonight," said Lila, starting off. "We have a proposal to make to you, and you all play a part. At this time, we would like to ask Becca and Curtis to pass out the prospectus."

Becca and Curtis got up and handed everyone at the table a sheet of paper with some writing and diagrams on it while Callum and Lila held up a large map. It showed an area at the edge of the National Forest. A plot of land had been highlighted with a thick red marker.

"Why, Luther, *look!*" cried Aunt Donaldina excitedly. "*That's our sanctuary!*"

"That's right, Aunt Donaldina," said Lila. "And what Callum and I propose is that you make it the Throckmorton-Gordon Sanctuary for the Gifted, Bright, and Perceptive Stray Dog."

"The *what?*" cried Aunt Donaldina, dumbfounded.

"The Throckmorton-Gordon Sanctuary for the Gifted, Bright, and Perceptive Stray Dog will be a haven for the poor lost canine souls that are presently roaming the streets of the city without any direction in life," explained Lila. "It will also be a learning ground, a teaching center, and an adoption-placement service."

"Oh, my goodness. That sounds lovely," said Mrs. Throckmorton, sounding relieved.

"It provides the sanctuary with a special use, which takes care of the snag," said Callum, as if to clinch the deal.

"As you can see from the prospectus," said Lila, "Curtis and Tito have sketched some design plans for the facility, and Becca and Rachel have outlined some programs and curricula."

"We did it today in life sciences," said Becca. "Mr. Sears is giving us credit for it."

"You did a wonderful job, guys," said Mr. Throckmorton. "I'm really impressed."

"As for faculty," said Callum. "I would like to ask my three friends from the park if they would like to help out."

Everyone looked at the three Grampas.

"*Us?*" cried the three Grampas, speaking as one.

"If you'd like to," said Callum.

"Are you kidding? I love the outdoors!" said Tom. "It's the only place where you can really appreciate the weather. Count me in."

"I love dogs," said Dick. "And I've always kind of felt like a stray myself. Count me in."

"What the heck," said Harry. "It sounds like a blast. I'll come. Pass me another of those delicious tacos, please."

"As for the program supervisor," said Callum, "I would like to nominate world-famous wildlife wrangler Buzz Optigon."

"It's an honor," said Buzz. "I can think of no better place to finish writing my memoirs. I'm getting pretty tired of staying at the zoo. The officials there are always breathing down my neck. Just tell me how to get there and when you want me."

"It certainly sounds like a *special use*," said Aunt Donaldina, thinking it over. "But *where* are we going to find enough *gifted*, *bright*, and *perceptive stray dogs*?"

Right on cue, there suddenly came a thunderous barking from outside.

Lila and Callum smiled at each other.

Everyone rushed from the table and ran out the front door. Gathered in front of the house was an enormous group of stray dogs. They spilled out into the street. They stopped traffic, both ways. And no one could get past on the sidewalk. But no one seemed to mind. Everyone was stunned because it was so unexpected a spectacle.

For a group made up of so many stray dogs, it was very well behaved. Every last one of them sat on their haunches patiently, as if waiting for something.

"*Well*," said Aunt Donaldina cautiously. "These dogs certainly look *gifted* and *bright*, but are they *perceptive*?"

"This is Aunt Donaldina," Callum said to the dogs. "She'll be the one running the place." Of course, the way he said it went something like "Bark! Woof! Yip, yap, *yippee!*"

The dogs all suddenly jumped to their feet and began grinning and wagging their tails as if they'd gone completely insane.

A tear came to Aunt Donaldina's eye. She held out her hands toward the grinning, wagging group.

"I hereby invite you *all*," she said grandly, "to join the *Throckmorton-Gordon Sanctuary for the Gifted, Bright, and Perceptive Stray Dog!*"

For some reason, that didn't need to be translated at all. The happy barking and yapping that commenced after that was so loud that it probably could have been heard as far off as the planet Mars.

CHAPTER TWENTY-ONE
Callum at Home

Glad to see you again," said Charlie the cabbie as Callum clambered into the backseat with Lila and Stanley Kramer. "To tell you the truth, I was beginning to think you'd run off and gotten yourself another cab instead of mine."

"It was nothing like that," said Callum quickly. He liked Charlie very much and certainly didn't want to hurt his feelings. "It's just that Ms. Mendez didn't allow me to come back to school until today."

"I'm glad she changed her mind," said Charlie. "Good for her. Sometimes it just takes a good night's sleep to see things more clearly. Am I right?"

"In this case," said Lila, "I think it was the award that Callum got from the mayor that did it. We both got one for the part that we played in the creation of the Throckmorton-Gordon Sanctuary for the Gifted, Bright, and Perceptive Stray Dog."

"Yes, I heard about that. It was all over the Internet," said Charlie. "If you ask me, I think it took the mayor long enough too. I was proud of you guys right from the start. Now if only someone will do something to help all of the stray *cats* around here."

Callum and Lila grinned at each other.

"We're working on it," said Lila. "There's plenty of room at the sanctuary. We just haven't figured out how to speak their language yet."

"I see you've got on a new Hargrove blazer," Charlie told Callum. "It fits you a lot better than the last one I saw you wearing."

"It d-d-does look g-g-good," stammered Stanley Kramer admiringly.

"Thanks, Stanley," said Callum. "Thanks, Charlie. It's my very own."

"So you're back in school for good then?" asked Charlie.

"I get to come three days a week and sit in on Lila's class in the Yellow Level," said Callum, and Stanley looked jealous enough to explode. "On Tuesdays, Thursdays, and Saturdays I have to meet with a tutor. I'm learning how to read and write and a lot of other things. There's a lot of homework."

"Take your time," said Charlie. "Learning is a wonderful thing. It's important to get it right. Some people never do. Take this jerk in the long, sleek black car up ahead of us, for example. He always parks in the middle of the street. You'd think he would have learned by now that no one is allowed to do that, am I right?"

"So," said Mr. Throckmorton later that night when the family was grouped around the dinner table. "How was everyone's day? I'll start first. Zoo officials have decided that the reason Tinto the genius painter elephant has been in a real funk is because he really wants to be a landscape designer and not an abstract artist, and so now they're going to let him rearrange the elephant habitat, and he seems absolutely delighted about it. It looks pretty sure that he'll never pick up a broom as a paintbrush in his genius trunk again. Which makes the Tinto masterpieces at the Metropolitan Art Gallery extremely rare, and we've sold every single one of them at prices that would make King Midas blush."

"I'm proud of you, dear," said Mrs. Throckmorton. "And I'm happy for Tinto."

"Good job, Dad," said Callum and Lila.

"Thank you," said Dad. "Now, what about you?"

"I'll go second," said Mom. "It turned out that I was right about the dinosaur bone being a leg bone after all, and when we put it where it belonged, everything else fell into place, and so our bossasaurus skeleton will be up for public viewing at the Science Academy next week."

"The head bone's connected to the neck bone," Dad began to sing. "The neck bone's connected to the . . ."

"*Shoulder bone!*" yelled Callum and Lila, and everyone laughed.

"The anatomy diagram really helped me," said Callum.

"Why can't anyone remember that there's no yelling at the dinner table?" said Dad after that. "For the umpteenth time, it's a house rule." Then he sighed and said, "I love that song."

"We know you do, dear," said Mom. "What about you two?" she asked Callum and Lila. "What happened in school today?"

"Billy Bankson's parents appeared out of nowhere right in the middle of math with Mr. Hervey," said Lila.

"Wow," said Dad. "I was beginning to think that they didn't exist."

"Now, dear," said Mom. "Don't interrupt. It's another house rule."

"Sorry, everybody," said Dad.

"They were furious with Billy," Lila went on. "We don't know what he did to deserve it, but it must have been something really awful. They took him out of class, and right in front of everyone they told him that they were sending him to a military academy where he would have to dig trenches and empty out latrines until he learned to be a responsible and productive member of society."

"Goodness," Mom said with a shudder. "That sounds a little harsh. But it might be just the thing he needs to get some discipline in life."

"If you ask me, that whole family should go to a military

academy and dig trenches and empty out latrines," said Dad. "The sooner, the better."

"And we voted for a class president today," said Callum. "Guess who won?"

"You?" guessed Dad.

"Lila?" guessed Mom.

"Roger Phipps," said Callum. "Jose Alvarez voted for him, and John Mason, of course, but so did Becca Adams and Rachel Cohen and Curtis Takahashi and Tito Jones and me."

"The whole class voted for him," said Lila. "No one even ran against him."

"He sounds like a popular guy," said Dad.

"He is," said Callum. "He's the Alpha Male of the Yellow Level. As far as the students go, that is."

"And I'm the Alpha Female," said Lila. "Along with Becca. Callum told me so."

"Well, don't get too big for your britches," said Mom. "There's only room for one Alpha Female in this family."

"And there's only room for one Alpha Male," said Dad. "So you two are stuck being Betas."

"Who's the Omega?" asked Callum.

"I suppose we can all take turns being the Omega from time to time," said Mom. "But let's not make it a competition or anything."

"May Callum and I be excused from the table now, please?" asked Lila.

"Don't you want dessert?" asked Mom. "We're having carrot cake."

"No ice cream?" said Lila.

"Your father and I are never eating ice cream again, if we can help it," said Mom.

"That's for sure," said Dad. "Not even if it's triple chunk, my favorite."

"We want to do our homework early so we can watch a special show about migratory birds on the Discovery Channel," said Lila.

"In that case, you may be excused," said Mom. "And I'd like to watch that show too. Rinse off your plates and put them into the dishwasher."

Lila and Callum did as they were told like the obedient Betas they were, and then Mom and Dad settled down with a nice piece of carrot cake to look through the mail.

Suddenly the peace and quiet was broken by a high-pitched noise that was so loud it seemed to shake the walls.

Mom and Dad raced upstairs. They found Lila and Callum in Lila's room. The lights were turned off. Callum and Lila were sitting on the floor in a bright patch of moonlight that was shining through the bedroom window. Outside, a quarter moon was on the rise, looking like a big happy smile in the sky.

"What's wrong?" Mom asked frantically.

"Are you injured?" asked Dad. "Was that a death cry?"

"We were howling at the rising moon," Lila explained in utter ecstasy.

"We had to," said Callum. "Look how big and bright it is, even though it's just a quarter full."

"It looks like it's smiling at us!" said Lila.

"Oh my," said Mom to Dad. "We don't have a house rule about howling at the rising moon yet, do we?"

"I think it's all right," said Dad. "As long as it's only on special occasions. What do you think?"

"Sounds good to me," said Mom. "I feel the lunar pull. Shall we?"

"We shall," said Dad.

And the whole family howled their lungs out at the rising moon.

ACKNOWLEDGMENTS

Special thanks to the following people, without whom I would still be scribbling away in total anonymity: my agent, Jennifer DeChiara, who called me up out of the blue one afternoon and changed my life for the better, in heartfelt appreciation of her friendship and business acumen; my editor, Margaret Miller, with whom I share a similar taste in children's lit and alternative rock, for her insight and big heart; artist Victor Rivas, for blessing this book with such a beautiful cover; my dad, for his loving support through thick and thin; Monica Scott, for her sage advice; Brian Power, for surviving our childhood battles without holding a grudge; Adam Hervey, for his indispensable technological assistance; Sheila Benson, for her early avid love for Callum; and the fine folks at Bloomsbury Children's Books who took this book under their wing, in gratitude for the care and attention they gave to it.

A million thanks also to the US Forest Service for its stewardship of the nation's forests and grasslands, upon which so much wildlife depends.

TIMOTHY POWER holds an art degree from California Institute of the Arts and has worked as a prop designer for Nickelodeon and other cartoon studios. He is currently a substitute teacher in Los Angeles. This is his first book.

www.timothypower.me

Mr. Cheeseman

and his three attractive, polite, relatively odor-free children are on the run. From what?

Well, that's a whole nother story. . . .

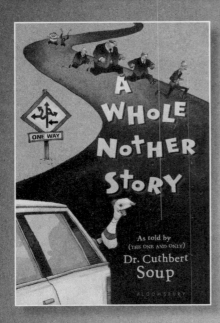

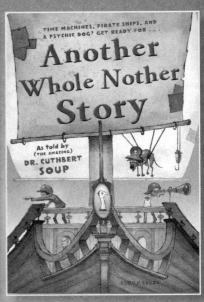

"If you take yourself very seriously, perhaps this isn't the book for you. But if you're in the mood for a lot of silliness and reading about a really interesting and quirky family, then it's perfect."

—Wired.com/GeekDad

www.awholenotherbook.com

BLOOMSBURY
CHILDREN'S
BOOKS

www.bloomsburykids.com